Camfield Place,
Hatfield
Hertfordshire,
England

Dearest Reader,

Camfield Novels of Love mark a very exciting era of my books with Jove. They have already published nearly two hundred of my titles since they became my first publisher in America, and now all my original paperback romances in the future will be published exclusively by them.

As you already know, Camfield Place in Hertfordshire is my home, which originally existed in 1275, but was rebuilt in 1867 by the grandfather of Beatrix Potter.

It was here in this lovely house, with the best view in the county, that she wrote *The Tale of Peter Rabbit*. Mr. McGregor's garden is exactly as she described it. The door in the wall that the fat little rabbit could not squeeze underneath and the goldfish pool where the white cat sat twitching its tail are still there.

I had Camfield Place blessed when I came here in 1950 and was so happy with my husband until he died, and now with my children and grandchildren, that I know the atmosphere is filled with love and we have all been very lucky.

It is easy here to write of love and I know you will enjoy the Camfield Novels of Love. Their plots are definitely exciting and the covers very romantic. They come to you, like all my books, with love.

Bless you,

Barbara Cartland

CAMFIELD NOVELS OF LOVE
by *Barbara Cartland*

Other books by *Barbara Cartland*

THE GOLDEN CAGE

"What happened to hurt you?" Mr. Thorpe asked quietly. With a jerk, Crisa realized that once again he had been reading her thoughts and was aware of what she was feeling.

"I . . . I cannot . . . talk about it," she said.

"Why not?"

She would have turned away, but he said, "Sit down, and talk to me for a moment. If you are nervous, so am I."

There was a plea in his voice that Crisa could not ignore.

Almost as if he ordered her to do so, she sat down again, looking at him with wide eyes, wondering how he could sense, for that must be the right word, so much about her . . .

"Tell me about yourself," he said. "Surely it is very strange for somebody as young as you are to be traveling without a chaperone, or somebody to look after you?"

"There is nothing to tell," she said quickly.

"That is not true," he answered.

Crisa looked at him, trying to find an answer, but finding it impossible . . .

A CAMFIELD NOVEL OF LOVE

by Barbara Cartland

"Barbara Cartland's novels are all distinguished by their intelligence, good sense, and good nature . . ."

—ROMANTIC TIMES

"Who could give better advice on how to keep your romance going strong than the world's most famous romance novelist, Barbara Cartland?"

—THE STAR

A NEW CAMFIELD NOVEL OF LOVE BY

BARBARA CARTLAND

The Golden Cage

A JOVE BOOK

THE GOLDEN CAGE

A Jove Book/published by arrangement with
the author

PRINTING HISTORY
Jove edition/December 1986

ISBN: 0-515-08795-5

Jove Books are published by The Berkley Publishing Group,
200 Madison Avenue, New York, N.Y. 10016. The words
"A JOVE BOOK" and the "J" with sunburst are trademarks
belonging to Jove Publications, Inc.

PRINTED IN THE UNITED STATES OF AMERICA

Author's Note

THE competition of the Ocean Liners from the 1870s on-wards resulted in revolutionary changes that astonished the world.

The *Dynamic* of 1883, built by Harland and Wolff for the Belfast Steamship Company, was one of the first vessels to be lighted throughout by electricity.

Passenger vessels were well ahead of the shore in the matter of electric lighting. It was not until 1887 that the Savoy was the first theatre to be lit by electricity, and the first electric street lamps did not appear until 1891.

It was a Cunarder, the *Lucania*, who became the first vessel to be in wireless touch with both sides of the Atlantic at once.

The French Line's *La Touraine* was slower but beautiful, and was the first liner to offer cabins *en suite*. Their food was better, although not quite so prolific as the *Cunard*, who advertised ten meals a day would be provided, which included a pint cup of bouillon, sandwiches carried about the deck, trays of ices at 3 P.M., and toffee and sweets at 5 P.M.

Macy's, one of the oldest of the great American Stores, added to their building in 1881 by putting up a six-storey addition extending Eastward of the existing quarters on 14th Street and completing the building during the first part of 1892.

Incorporated in it was a new Ladies Waiting Room, which they described as "the most beautiful and luxurious department devoted to the comfort of ladies to be found in a mercantile establishment in the city. The style of decoration is Louis XV and no expense has been spared."

chapter one

1896

CRISA went to the window and looked out onto Fifth Avenue.

She did not see the traffic trotting by beneath her, or the huge ugly brown-stone houses which faced the enormous creamy limestone mansion built in imitation of the lilting grace of the *châteaux* of the Loire Valley by Silas P. Vanderhault when he married his first wife.

Instead, she was seeing the ancient Manor House, where the Roydens had lived in Huntingdonshire since James I had created the first Baronet.

Although it had been badly in need of restoration, the red bricks in need of painting, the wood of the gables rotten, and many panes missing from the windows, she thought then, as she did now, it was the most beautiful place on earth.

She longed for it with a yearning that was like an aching wound in her heart.

Now she had lost both the Manor and her father, who had been the last Baronet, and, she thought dismally, her youth.

Sometimes she had thought that in the over-luxuriant atmosphere, the crowded streets, and the eternal bustling of New York, she had grown old overnight, although it was only last week that she had celebrated her nineteenth birthday.

Only nineteen! And yet she felt she had lived nineteen centuries since she had married Silas P. Vanderhault and become the third wife of one of the richest men in America.

Even now she could hardly believe it, and that he, too, like her father, was dead.

She could remember so well the day it had all happened.

She had been out riding, alone because ever since her mother's death her father, as if he could not bear to remain in the house where they had been so happy, had been continually going to London.

She had known each time he returned that he had not only spent his time drinking and eating too much, which was bad for his health, but he had also spent more money than they could possible afford.

He would then come home because, as he himself had said often enough, he was "completely and absolutely broke."

This time he had been away for nearly two weeks and Crisa was not expecting him, when she saw as she neared the house a smart travelling-carriage outside the front door.

Her heart leapt with delight, although as she drew nearer to it she had a feeling of dismay that her father should have been so extravagant in hiring such an expensive carriage drawn by what she recognised as fine and extremely well-bred horses.

"How can he be so foolish as to come home in such style," she asked herself, "when we already owe Lovett's an astronomical amount?"

Lovett's was the nearest livery stables, from which her father usually hired a Post Chaise to take him to London and which he invariably complained was uncomfortable and slow, though the trains were worse.

This was a quite different turn-out, and as Crisa walked into the stables to hand her horse over to old Hodges, who moved very slowly because of his rheumatism, she decided she would talk to her father very seriously, now that he was home, about their financial affairs.

Last week she had found it embarrassing to go down to the village because she thought that the small shopkeepers, even though they loved her, would look at her reproachfully when she ordered more goods.

They knew she was unable to pay so much as a few pence for a pound of the flour, sugar, or the butter that Nanny required.

Nanny was far more voluble on the subject than anyone else.

"What's your father going to do about us, I'd like to know?" she had said only last night. "'Twas with great difficulty that I managed to persuade Mr. Goodgson up at the farm to kill a cockerel for us to eat. The Lord knows the poor bird was so old it could hardly walk, but even so he was asking two shillings for it, and when I tells him to put it on our account, he almost threw it at me!"

Crisa sighed, knowing she had no answer to this, and Nanny knew it too.

"If only your father understood that we can't live on grass, and if I've to go through another winter without any coal, it's doubtful if I'll survive, and when I'm dead he'll be sorry!"

Crisa had given a choked little laugh and put her arms around Nanny to say:

"Do not dare talk of dying, Nanny! You know perfectly well you have to stay alive and look after me."

She kissed the old woman on the cheek before she went on:

"I will talk to Papa when he comes back, I really will. But you know how unhappy he has been since Mama died, and I know by the look in his eyes how much he misses her. He feels he cannot stay here and not see her come smiling into a room, so happy to be with him."

Crisa's voice broke on the words because she had loved her mother deeply and found it just as hard to live without her as her father did.

But she had not the solace of being able to go away and spend money they had not got.

"It's sinful," Nanny had once said scathingly, "going with those Gaiety Girls, and riff-raff of that sort!"

"They are all supposed to be very beautiful and very unusual—at least that is what the newspapers say," Crisa argued.

"Now, don't you go putting more ideas into your father's head than he's got there already," Nanny admonished.

Crisa had thought it tactful not to question her father too closely as to what he did when he went to London.

At the same time, she knew that every day he was there added to their pile of debts, and every time he returned it seemed to make him more depressed and more restless than he had been the time before.

At least, she thought as she walked up to the house, she could see him, she could talk to him, and when he was not there, she was very lonely without him.

There was only Nanny grumbling, old Hodges complaining about his rheumatism, and her only consolation was the horses she could ride.

As she entered the hall, with its pictures of the Royden ancestors on the walls and the carpet which had grown so threadbare that it was impossible to see the pattern, she wondered where her father would be.

Then she heard voices in the Drawing-Room, which meant he had brought somebody with him.

She wondered whether she should go upstairs and change or go in to join them just as she was in her old faded riding-skirt with which, as it was warm, she was wearing only a white blouse which had been darned in a number of places and patched at the elbows.

Then she told herself that whoever had returned with her father would not notice her.

She had pushed open the Drawing-Room door and saw him at the far end of the room talking to another man.

With a cry of joy that he was back she ran towards him, flinging her arms around his neck.

"You are home, Papa!" she exclaimed. "Why did you not let me know you were coming? I would have been here waiting for you."

"I only decided at the last moment, my Poppet," he answered, "and when I arrived, Nanny told us, as I expected, that you had gone riding."

"I was wishing you were with me," Crisa said, taking her arms from around his neck and looking enquiringly at the man standing beside him.

He was shorter than her father and she thought he looked old and not very attractive.

His hair, what was left of it, was grey, his face was deeply lined, and his clothes seemed a little odd and not exactly what she expected a gentleman to wear.

"Let me introduce you," Sir Robert Royden was saying. "Mr. Vanderhault—this is my daughter, Crisa."

"And a very beautiful possession too!" Mr. Vanderhault said as Crisa held out her hand.

He had a strong nasal accent, and even if her father had not explained where he came from, Crisa would have known he was an American.

"Mr. Vanderhault has come down with me from London in order to see our Van Dycks," her father explained.

Crisa drew in her breath, and with the greatest difficulty prevented herself from giving a cry of horror.

She knew exactly what her father meant by bringing the American home.

After all his promises, after all he had said, he intended to sell the only two valuable possessions they had left, the Van Dyck portraits of the first Roydens, who had graced the Court of Charles I and taken the Royden name into the history books.

Her mother had loved both the pictures and she had often said to her husband:

"Whatever else we may sell, darling, we must never

6

part with our Van Dycks. They are so much a part of our lives that I always feel I know them."

"I feel the same," Sir Robert had said, "and you are quite right, darling. Even if we do not have a son to inherit the Baronetcy, Crisa will carry on the family name, and perhaps when she has a son she will call him Royden."

"I will certainly do that," Crisa had promised.

At the same time, she was well aware how bitterly her father regretted that with him the Baronetcy, which had passed so many times from father to son, would come to an end.

When her mother died, although she had never dared to say it aloud, she had wondered whether her father would marry again, hoping to get the longed-for heir which her mother had been unable to give him.

She knew how much it had hurt her mother to feel she had failed somebody she loved as passionately as she loved her husband.

Once when she had been unaware that Crisa was listening, her mother had said:

"I wonder if you will ever forgive me, darling, for not giving you a son."

Her father had laughed, and it had been a genuine sound.

"You have given me a happiness which is far more important than anything else that a man could ask for," he had replied, "and I love our precious daughter because she looks like you."

Yet, Crisa had known as the years went by that he would often look at the family portraits, none of which were in the least valuable except for the Van Dycks, and pain filled his eyes because he knew there was nobody else except herself to inherit them, and if she married, her name would not be Royden.

Yet now, after all his promises to her mother and to her, she knew without being told that the Van Dycks had to go.

"I have been telling Mr. Vanderhault as we came down here," her father was saying, "the story of the Royden family, and how my ancestors fought with Marlborough and at the Battle of Waterloo, besides providing at the beginning of the century one of the Statesmen in Queen Victoria's first Cabinet."

If she had not been so horrified at what he was going to do, Crisa would have been amused at knowing her father had picked out for the American periods of history of which he was likely to have heard.

She knew there were other ancestors who had always intrigued her father far more, one of whom had been an explorer acclaimed as one of the few men ever to find the source of the Amazon.

Another had made a name for himself during the wars in India under Sir Arthur Wellesley.

However, even an American, she thought scathingly, would have heard of the famous Duke of Marlborough, and would know that the Battle of Waterloo had been the final defeat for Napoleon Bonaparte.

"If there's one thing I enjoy," Mr. Vanderhault replied, "it's taking back to America some of the fine old treasures that are available in this great little country of yours."

That was true enough, Crisa was to think later when she saw the Vanderhault house in New York, and found that an inordinate amount of pictures and furniture had been grouped together without any artistic sense.

There were Egyptian mummy-cases, rugs smothering

rugs, bookcases, tables, vases, figurines, and china, all of which packed closely one against another had a nightmare quality which was overwhelming.

Now she found it impossible to say anything as her father led the way to the other end of the Drawing-Room, where the Van Dycks were hanging on either side of the mantelpiece.

In the winter they sat at this end of the room, but in the summer at the other end, where a French window opened into the rose garden which centred around an ancient sun-dial.

The Van Dycks were, Crisa thought as she looked up at them, so exquisitely painted and so beautiful in themselves, that it seemed impossible that her father could contemplate having them removed and taken out of the house.

The walls of the Manor had been their background for centuries, and it was as if they belonged there as much as he did himself.

Her eyes did not miss how Van Dyck with his genius had depicted the elegant drapery of Charlotte Royden's gown and his inimitable touch in showing the long thin fingers of her husband.

In the background of both pictures stood the Manor, looking just as it did today, but not in need of repair.

"You can see how fine they are," Sir Robert remarked, "no one before or since Van Dyck could paint portraits as well as he did."

Mr. Vanderhault nodded, but Crisa had the uncomfortable feeling that his eyes, old though they might be, did not miss the fact that both the pictures needed cleaning, and there was a small tear in the canvas of Charlotte Royden's portrait.

"Of course, if you are not interested," Sir Robert was

saying, "I know the National Gallery will be, but I had not thought until a day or so ago of disposing of portraits which have been in my family for so many generations and have hung in this house for more than two hundred and fifty years."

Crisa drew in her breath.

She could not bear to hear her father talking like a salesman, though she knew him well enough to know that he was hating what he had to do.

He was being forced into it by circumstances he had not yet admitted to her.

Then she started, because she suddenly realised that Mr. Vanderhault was not looking at the portraits, but at her.

"And what do you think, Miss Crisa?" he asked. "I would like to hear your opinion."

"I love both the portraits," Crisa replied in a low voice, "and I think it will break my heart to lose them."

"I guessed that was what you would say."

He did not say any more, but abruptly, which seemed rather strange, he walked back to the other side of the room, where he had put down the drink he had been holding in his hand when Sir Robert had taken him to look at the portraits.

Crisa was aware that her father gave her a frantic glance, as if he thought what she had said would upset a prospective buyer.

Then to the astonishment of both Crisa and her father, Mr. Vanderhault said:

"I wonder, Sir Robert, if it would inconvenience you if I stayed here the night? It has been a long journey from London, and I would really appreciate staying in a real English home and having a chance while I am here of looking at your other pictures."

Crisa could still remember what a commotion it had caused.

It was not only Mr. Vanderhault who had to be accommodated, but also the coachman, and what had appeared to be a footman on the box but turned out to be his secretary, who always travelled with him wherever he went.

It meant that Nanny, who did the cooking, had to provide a dinner for three in the Dining-Room, dinner for the secretary Mr. Krissam, who ate alone, and supper for the coachman, who needless to say was far more hungry than anyone else.

Only with Crisa's help, and with old Hodges having to dig the vegetables from the garden because she had no time, and the coachman being sent to purchase food from the village, did they manage to have what Sir Robert thought privately was a somewhat scanty meal.

Mr. Vanderhault, however, seemed quite content with everything that was put in front of him and to appreciate the excellent claret of which there were only a few bottles left and kept for very special occasions.

All the time they were eating he talked incessantly of his possessions in America, of his ownership of one of the great railways springing up in the West, and his good fortune in striking oil on the land he owned in Texas.

In fact, it was difficult for anybody else to speak except Mr. Vanderhault, who had so much to say.

Crisa was wondering how her father could have found an American like him in the Theatres, the Night-Clubs, and the Restaurants, where he enjoyed himself in London.

She had been thankful when after dinner her father had suggested that she should go to bed early.

"Mr. Vanderhault and I have a great deal of business to talk over, my dearest," he had said. "So I suggest you pop off to bed, and I will tell you all about it tomorrow."

Crisa guessed he wished to haggle with Mr. Vanderhault about the price of the Van Dycks and would feel embarrassed if she were listening.

She therefore kissed her father good-night, and holding out her hand to Mr. Vanderhault, said:

"Good-night, Mr. Vanderhault, and I hope you enjoy your stay in England."

"That's one of the things I'm going to talk about to your father," he replied.

To her surprise he held her hand in both of his as he went on:

"You are a very lovely girl, and a real honey, as we say back home. It's a shame you have to sell the treasures that belong to you instead of having them laid at your feet by men who will love you because you are so beautiful."

It was such a surprise to hear an old man talk like that Crisa was embarrassed, but she merely smiled at him prettily and said:

"Thank you for saying such nice things to me."

She had a little difficulty in freeing her hand from his, and then with a last loving glance at her father she left the Drawing-Room and went upstairs to her own room.

She knew without being told that her father would come and say good-night to her when finally she heard him and Mr. Vanderhault coming upstairs.

The American was shown into what was always known as "The Queen Anne Room," although it was doubtful if the Queen had ever slept there.

Then, as Crisa expected, she heard her father walking down the passage and as he opened the door she sat up in bed.

He came towards her and she thought he was looking very serious, and at the same time as handsome as he always did.

She thought, as she had at dinner, that the contrast between the two men was almost ludicrous.

Mr. Vanderhault might be rich, but his money was unable to help his lined face and his sagging chin, which did not fit well into the stiff collar, which she fancied was a size too small for him.

Her father, lithe, athletic, and looking smart despite the fact that his evening-clothes were, as she knew only too well, almost threadbare and should have been replaced years ago, sat down on the side of her bed.

He looked at her as if he had never seen her before.

"Has he . . . bought the . . . Van Dycks, Papa?" Crisa asked in a whisper.

She knew the answer. At the same time, almost like the voice of doom, she knew she had to hear it to make it quite certain.

"He made me a proposition, Crisa, but I hardly know how to tell you about it."

There was so much pain in Sir Robert's voice that Crisa put out her hand and slipped it into his.

"I am sorry, Papa," she said, "I know what you are feeling. But we cannot go on without money. We have to pay the people in the village or else sit here and starve."

"I know," Sir Robert agreed heavily, "but Mr. Vanderhault has the answer to all that."

"All I hope is that you got a good price for the Van Dycks."

Her father drew in his breath, then he said:

"He is prepared to give me thirty thousand pounds, which as you are aware will clear up all our debts and provide an income of three thousand pounds a year for the rest of my life!"

Crisa looked at her father in sheer astonishment, feeling she could not have heard him aright.

"Thirty thousand pounds and three thousand a year for life?" she repeated as though she must have misunderstood him. "All that for the Van Dycks?"

"And—for you!" Sir Robert said quietly.

For a moment there was just silence.

Then Crisa asked in a voice that did not sound like her own:

"Wh-what are you . . . saying, Papa? I . . . I do not understand."

"Mr. Vanderhault wishes to marry you," Sir Robert replied. "He said that the moment he saw you he knew you were what he had been seeking ever since he had become a widower five years ago."

He shut his eyes and drew in his breath before he said:

"He is prepared to settle on you a million dollars the day you marry him and to leave you when he dies a millionairess a dozen times over!"

"I . . . I do not believe it!" Crisa said. "I do not . . . believe it is . . . possible!"

Then before her father could speak she said:

"Of course I could not marry an . . . old man like that!

Someone I have seen only for a few hours! How can he think of anything so . . . horrible, so . . . impossible?"

But even as she spoke she had known by the expression on her father's face that it was what she had to do.

"I cannot . . . I cannot do it . . . Papa," she said over and over again as he sat on her bed talking about it until the dawn broke.

When finally Sir Robert left her to go to his own room, Crisa had known it was something she had to do and that there was no escape.

Her father had told her reluctantly and shamefacedly that his debts in London and his overdraft at the Bank had grown to such proportions that unless something was done and quickly, there was every likelihood of his being arrested.

"If I shot myself, the bailiffs would seize everything I possess," he said, "including this house and its contents, and you would be left to starve. It is impossible for me to make any provision for you."

Crisa had not spoken, and he continued:

"I was in despair when suddenly a friend at the Club introduced me to Mr. Vanderhault, saying:

" 'I believe you have some rather fine pictures, Robert, of the sort that Mr. Vanderhault is looking for to take home to America.'

"I had already told myself," Sir Robert went on, "that I would have to find a purchaser for the Van Dycks, and it seemed as if it was a deliberate intervention of Fate that he should be brought to me without any trouble."

"And he . . . really wants to . . . marry me?" Crisa asked in a low voice.

"He wants before he dies to have a son," Sir Robert

answered. "He has had four daughters by his two wives, but neither of them gave him a son."

Crisa felt herself shiver, and although she was very innocent and had no idea what love-making meant between a man and a woman, at the same time, the idea of that old American touching her made her want to run away and hide.

It was a feeling that she had again and again during the next week, and yet incredibly, yet inevitably, by the end of it she was the wife of Silas P. Vanderhault and they were on their way to America.

Nothing had seemed real from the moment she walked up the aisle of their village Church on her father's arm to see the little man, with his wrinkled face, waiting for her at the altar-steps.

Her fingers were cold as he put the gold wedding-ring on her finger and repeated in a nasal accent after the Clergyman the words which made her his wife.

There had been a very small luncheon-party at the Manor, a wedding-cake cooked and decorated by Nanny, and champagne provided by Mr. Vanderhault with which everybody drank their health.

Only when they drove to the nearest station to catch a train to Liverpool, where they would board an American Liner to carry them to New York, did Crisa think she was not dreaming but having a nightmare.

This man sitting beside her, talking about himself and his possessions, was her husband. He had paid for her more money than she had ever dreamt of, but for her that was no compensation for being his.

She had known how much it had hurt her father to see her go, but the contracts which Mr. Vanderhault had signed after the ceremony in the presence of his Solicitor, who had come down from London and was one of the guests at the wedding, were lying on her father's desk.

If her life had changed from the moment the ring had gone onto her finger, so had her father's.

He was now a rich man, and she was quite certain that when she had gone, he would not stay at the Manor, but would rush back to London in the hope that the Gaiety Girls, the Night-Clubs and the Restaurants of which Nanny talked so scathingly would be efficacious in making him forget—forget that he had not only lost the wife he loved, but also sold his daughter who meant so much to him.

It was only when they reached Liverpool, boarded the ship, and had been ushered into two State Rooms overwhelmingly decorated with lilies and orchids that Crisa knew the bars of gold which constituted her prison were closing around her.

She was to be conscious of them from that moment, as if she could actually see them walling her in.

Her husband was still talking, still telling her how he had ordered the Shipping Line, in which of course he was a large shareholder, to provide the very best for himself and his bride.

She realised that it had been Mr. Krissam who had seen to every detail—the flowers, the huge baskets of exotic fruits she was sure they would never eat, the pots of caviar, and the apparently endless bottles of champagne which appeared to be taken away almost as soon as they were opened.

Silas P. Vanderhault was in a triumphant mood and had invited a large variety of people to their State Rooms as soon as they had boarded to come and drink their health and wish them good luck.

There was the Captain, the Purser, the Officers and

17

the stewards, all of whom were offered champagne, which they drank with relish, at the same time looking at her, she thought, as if they knew exactly how she had sold herself at the altar for the money this millionaire could give her.

It was not only money, for already he had showered her with presents when he returned from London for their wedding.

There was a huge diamond necklace which she privately thought was vulgar and far too large and heavy for her small neck.

There were diamond bracelets which seemed to weigh down her wrists, and not only an engagement-ring the size of a florin, but also a set of turquoises and diamonds in velvet boxes.

There was, too, a necklace of pearls which were so large and overpowering that she was sure if she wore them people would laugh.

She, however, thanked him politely and he said, patting her arm:

"Nothing's too good for the wife of Silas P. Vanderhault, and I can tell you, honey, when they see you in New York wearing these jewels, their eyes will pop out of their heads with envy!"

For a moment Crisa wanted to ask him if he expected her to wear them all at once, then she knew it was the sort of question Mr. Vanderhault would not think at all funny.

She had already learnt that he had very little sense of humour, although he did laugh at his own jokes.

More people came into the State Room to drink the champagne, and when finally they sat down to dinner in their other State Room, there were still passengers coming aboard, who on hearing that Mr. Vanderhault was sailing and celebrating his marriage, claimed an acquaintance with him.

The toasts went on until the ship sailed at midnight, and when Crisa thought that at last she could go to bed, she left her husband still drinking, still talking, and crept away.

Because she was apprehensive that the moment had come that she would be a married woman and the wife of a man she had hardly spoken to, she felt a cold shiver as she undressed.

She got into the big brass bedstead, conscious as she did so of the overwhelming fragrance of lilies that decorated the room.

Their Suite was fitted out in mahogany with everything to match, and there were hanging wardrobes from which on Mr. Krissam's instructions stewards had already unpacked what she would need for the voyage, and he had also had taken away the leather trunks so that they would not clutter up the cabin.

On her bed there was a nightgown that she and Nanny had bought in Huntingdon, and she felt because it was a finer material and decorated with lace that she had not been able to afford in the past, that it was somehow immodest and embarrassed her.

Because her father had made it very clear to Mr. Vanderhault that if she was to be married so quickly it would be impossible to collect a trousseau, a profusion of clothes that she had never imagined buying or owning was sent down from London by, she knew, Mr. Krissam from one of the most expensive and exclusive shops in Bond Street.

She had not bothered to try them on during her last days at the Manor.

Instead, she had ridden with her father every possible

hour of the day, knowing that only by feeling she was alone with him and they were riding together over the estate they loved could she prevent herself from crying out in horror at what lay ahead of her in the future.

As if he understood, they talked of everything but her forthcoming marriage, and only when she put on her wedding-gown did she realise that she would not only feel different as the wife of Silas P. Vanderhault, but would look different.

Her wedding-gown was indeed beautiful, but while Nanny exclaimed over it and she had even seen a glint of admiration in her father's eyes, she could hardly bother to look at herself in the mirror.

The same applied to her going-away dress with which there was a cape in case it was cold at sea, trimmed with the finest and most expensive sable.

The hat she knew came from a Milliner she had read about in the Ladies Fashion Magazine which Nanny occasionally borrowed from the Vicar's wife.

Her gloves were of such fine kid that she was almost afraid to put them on, and for the first time in her life she wore real silk stockings.

Now, as she finished undressing and put on her nightgown, she felt her heart beating in heavy strokes, almost as if a clock were ticking away the minutes she had to live.

For one frantic moment she wondered what would happen if she ran away as she wanted to do, if she went up on deck and threw herself over the rails into the sea.

They must be out of harbour by now, and darkness had fallen, so it would be very difficult to rescue her.

Then she knew that while she was afraid of her husband, she was just as afraid of dying in a way which she knew her father would think dishonourable, since they had already accepted so much from Silas P. Vander-hault.

Lying back against the pillows, she shut her eyes and thought of how her father would now be able to fill the stables with the young, well-bred, and spirited horses he had always longed to possess.

The house would be redecorated, the threadbare carpets and tattered curtains replaced, and before she left, Nanny had already engaged three maids to work in the house and two young girls from the village to help in the kitchen.

'Papa will be comfortable,' Crisa thought.

Yet she knew he would find the loneliness unbearable and would be more often in London than in Hunting-donshire.

Then she heard a movement outside her door and she felt a shiver of fear run through her.

This was the moment when her husband would come to her and she supposed, although she did not know what it meant, that he would make love to her.

She felt herself tremble as she waited, remembering suddenly that he had never kissed her on the lips.

But really there had not been time, and when he greeted her in front of her father, he had merely kissed her on the cheek, and even then she had felt his mouth was cold and his lips withered with age.

"I cannot bear it . . . I cannot!" Crisa cried to herself.

The door opened and she drew in her breath, stifling a little scream.

But it was not her husband who stood there silhouetted against the light from the State Room, but Mr. Krissam.

She stared at him in astonishment and he said:

"I'm sorry to tell you, Mrs. Vanderhault, but something terrible has happened!"

"What is it?" Crisa asked in a whisper.

"Mr. Vanderhault has had a collapse. I only hope it's nothing serious, but I've got him to bed, and the doctor is with him."

There was a pause before Crisa managed to ask:

"Shall . . . I come and . . . see him?"

"There's no point in doing so, Mrs. Vanderhault, since he's unconscious and won't know you're there. It would be best for you to stay where you are."

"Very well," Crisa managed to say, "but . . . will you please tell me . . . at once if I am . . . wanted?"

"Yes, of course, Mrs. Vanderhault, and I hope you'll be able to sleep and that things will be better in the morning."

Mr. Krissam closed the door and Crisa lay back and shut her eyes.

She could hardly believe what had happened was true, but she was alone—alone on her wedding-night! Alone and, for this night, at any rate, she was safe from what she dreaded with every nerve of her body.

chapter two

IT was Mr. Krissam who organised everything.

He arranged for somebody to be always in attendance on Mr. Vanderhault as he lay unconscious in his State Room, and Crisa learned from the doctor that he had in fact suffered a severe stroke.

She was left with nothing to do except sit in her own Room, reading the magazines which Mr. Krissam had supplied before they left England, and books from the ship's Library.

Twice a day she walked around the deck because she thought it was what she should do, but she was too shy to speak to anybody, or to make conversation with those who bade her a friendly "Good-Morning" or "Good-Afternoon."

She therefore had no contact with the outside world,

and when they reached New York, she was in fact over-whelmed by her introductions into American life, where she had never seen before anyone she met.

It was, needless to say, Mr. Krissam who introduced her to the huge house and to her husband's relatives, who were all waiting to meet her.

It took her all her time to sort out who they were. The most prominent amongst them, whose name was Matilda, and who was her husband's elder sister, an-nounced that she had moved in so as to keep her com-pany.

"I will show you the ropes," she said firmly.

This Crisa soon realised meant that Matilda was in charge of everything, and she was only a guest in her husband's house.

There were a great number of Silas Vanderhault's other relatives as well, including his four daughters, who were all married with families, and another sister, Anna, who was younger than Matilda, but still seemed to Crisa very old and very dictatorial.

They made it clear to her from the very beginning that things must go on in exactly the same way as they had before her arrival, and that nothing could be changed without her husband's authority.

As he was incapable of giving it, it was obvious that Crisa had no say in anything.

Every night when she went to bed alone in the huge, overfurnished, overdecorated bedroom she would cry, because she was so homesick and lonely, with a pas-sionate longing that was like a physical pain to be with her father.

She wrote to him every day and told him what was happening, but she deliberately did not ask him to come to her, feeling that even if he did so, there would be very little he could do.

She was certain he would hate the big, ugly house and the domineering Vanderhaults, and that would only make things worse than they were already.

Because she had so much freedom, living at home, and had been used to making her own decisions, at least about herself, she had to fight back the protests that came to her lips as every moment of the day she was instructed to do this or that.

She was taken to meet people, to see sights, to shop, whether she wished to do so or not, and she soon realised that Matilda and Anna had disliked their brother's first two wives, and their feelings where she was concerned were very much the same.

They resented her because she was English, because she was young, and because she was very much prettier than either of them or any of the other Vanderhault relations.

"How can I go on living like this?" Crisa asked herself a million times, and found no answer to the question.

Then, after she had been in New York for eight months, she learned that her father had been killed in a riding accident.

She could hardly believe it was true and that she would never see him again, and she wished despairingly that she had been brave enough to refuse to marry Silas Vanderhault and had stayed with her father to the end.

It was one of the new horses, which, as he told her in his letters, were giving him so much pleasure, that had thrown him unexpectedly when he was jumping a brick wall, and he had fallen awkwardly and broken his neck.

At the same time she knew from her father's letters that he had enjoyed being able to spend money on restoring the house and refurnishing many of the rooms. There was also no doubt that he was enjoying himself in London.

When they heard of her father's death, the Vanderhaults commiserated with her, but when she said she wished to return to England, they made it impossible for her to do so.

They pointed out that she would be too late anyway to attend his funeral, and that her place, although she could not communicate with him in any way, was at her husband's side.

Everything had been arranged, of course, by Mr. Krissam, with a smooth-running perfection with which nobody could find fault.

Nurses came in shifts and Mr. Vanderhault was never alone at any time. Doctors visited him daily, to go away saying there was nothing they could do, but obviously charging a huge fee for saying it.

His rooms, like the rest of the house, were filled with exotic hot-house flowers, and Crisa knew when she visited him there was nothing she could do for his comfort, and nothing he could do for her.

The clothes, and there were a great number of them by this time, which she had bought because she had nothing else to do and the Vanderhault women enjoyed going shopping with her, were because they were in colours all put on one side.

Instead, she bought an entirely new wardrobe of black, more because it was expected of her than because her father would have approved.

"If there is one thing I dislike," he had often said, "it

is seeing women looking like crows. At the same time, dearest, with your white skin and fair hair, black makes you look very theatrical."

He had said this to her after her mother's death, and because it was therefore unnecessary to keep wearing black at home in the Manor, she had after a month discarded her black gowns and worn ordinary clothes.

As she had spent most of the day in her riding-habit, which was an indeterminate grey, it was quiet enough if she was seen by their neighbours for them not to think it peculiar.

In New York, however, the Vanderhaults insisted on her purchasing black day gowns trimmed with crêpe, and black lace dresses for the evening ornamented with jet.

Because it was easier to agree than disagree, Crisa did what was required and, because she was so desperately unhappy about her father, thought it really of very little consequence how she looked.

Then a month after her father's death, Silas died in his sleep.

He had never regained consciousness, and in consequence, as he had been an almost impersonal figure for so long, Crisa found the weeping and mourning amongst his family somewhat inappropriate.

There was now beneath the dramatic behaviour of the crowds of relatives who came to the house before the funeral, an undercurrent of, Crisa thought, anxiety, and a quite obvious suspicion of her.

It took her a little time to understand what she felt perceptively rather than from anything they said.

Then she realised that they were all apprehensive about Silas's Will.

It was only after a very elaborate funeral, attended by everyone of any importance in New York, with a cortège of carriages stretching for over half a mile, that Crisa knew the "Day of Reckoning" had to be postponed before they would learn how Silas had distributed his money.

She was vaguely aware at the back of her mind that he had made a new Will when he married her.

This was confirmed when Matilda told her with a harsh note in her voice that unlike what was traditional, her brother's Will would not be read after the funeral because they were awaiting the arrival of his Solicitor from England.

"Why do we have to wait for him?" Crisa asked.

Matilda had given a laugh which Crisa thought was one of distinct enmity before she replied:

"As if you did not know!"

"Know what?"

"That we have learnt that my brother made certain arrangements for you when he married you in that hurried manner, and the documents have to be brought to New York."

"I had no idea that you would want them brought here," Crisa said simply, "but I do know there were some documents which he signed with Papa and his Solicitor after we had returned from the Church."

She saw by the expression on Matilda's face that she thought, and it was understandable, that Crisa had deliberately married her brother for his money, and would have extracted from him everything she possibly could.

There was some truth in that, Crisa thought miserably, but there was nothing she could do about it, nor could she say honestly, as she would have liked to do, that she had loved her husband for himself.

She could recall all too easily hearing herself pleading with her father not to have to marry "that old man," and she could remember her feelings of relief on the ship when he was incapable of making her his wife and giving her, as he had hoped, a son to inherit his vast millions.

"What is the use of the money now that Papa is dead?" she asked herself unhappily when she was alone in her room.

She had already received a letter from her father's Solicitor, Mr. Smithson, telling her he had left her everything he possessed, including the Manor. Mr. Smithson had also opened an account for her with a considerable sum of money in the Bank her father had always used.

It was there, waiting for her anytime she required it.

'If only I could go home,' she thought.

She told herself that now Silas was dead there was nothing to stop her, although it was obvious she could not announce immediately after his death that she intended to leave.

Then, eight days later, Matilda told her the Solicitor had arrived and there would be a meeting held in the Library, where her husband's Will would be read.

"Then," Matilda said sharply, "we shall all know where we stand."

It was on the tip of Crisa's tongue to say that as far as she was concerned, she did not want his money, and all she required was a ticket back to England, where she would be able to look after herself.

Then because she had worried over her father's finances, she remembered that now he was dead he would obviously not receive the 3,000 pounds a year that Silas had promised him.

She would, therefore, be wise to keep some money, at any rate, for herself; enough to ensure that the Manor did not again fall into disrepair, and that she would never be in debt as her father had to the point where he was, if it were true, threatened with imprisonment.

One thing she thought the Vanderhaults could certainly keep when she went home was this house, with its appalling collection of what Silas had called treasures, overcrowded and jostling against each other until they made her feel as if she had eaten too much *pâté de foie gras,* or had a mental indigestion from contemplating so many masterpieces packed like sardines in the velvet-curtained, overdecorated rooms.

Wearing one of her black gowns which Silas's oldest daughter had helped her choose, she went to the meeting in the Library, hoping, because she knew how much they would resent it, that Silas had not left her too much.

She could remember her father saying he had made a promise of what he would leave her after he was dead, but because then she had been so much concerned with living with him, she had not listened, even though she knew he was an old man.

As she expected, the room was packed with Vanderhault relatives, and she thought as she entered that they all eyed her in a hostile manner which made her feel very uncomfortable.

Only Anna's son, a young man called Dale, who was twenty-two, rose to meet her at the door. Crisa guessed it was on his mother's instructions that he took her along the room to where, seated at a table facing the throng of relatives, was Mr. Vanderhault's Solicitor from London, besides three partners from the firm who represented him in New York.

The four men rose as Crisa joined them, and Dale took it upon himself to introduce them by name before, having shaken their hands, she sat down in a chair allotted to her beside the Solicitors at the table where they sat.

She thought it was a strange arrangement, but was not prepared to argue about it.

She did, however, feel uncomfortable because she was facing all her husband's relatives, and she thought that now she was seated, they deliberately looked away from her, as if they did not wish to be accused of being too inquisitively avaricious.

There was a pencil and a small pad in front of her on which she supposed she was expected to make notes.

Instead, as the Solicitor started speaking, she began to doodle, conscious that it gave her an excuse for bending her head and not looking at the relatives listening attentively to every word.

"I much regret," the Solicitor was saying in his crisp English voice, "that I was unable to be here for the funeral of my most respected client, Mr. Silas P. Vanderhault, and I can only regret his untimely demise. When I last saw him so happy and apparently so well, it was on the occasion of his marriage to Miss Crisa Royden."

As he spoke her name, everybody in the room looked at Crisa who, anticipating that was what they would do, bent her head a little lower, still apparently writing on the pad in front of her.

"I will now read the last Will and Testament of Mr.

Silas P. Vanderhault," the English Solicitor went on, "which was signed by him on his wedding day, July 8th, 1895."

He then began to read in a dull, unemotional voice:

"I, Silás P. Vanderhault, being of sound mind, do hereby declare that this is my last Will and Testament..."

His voice seemed to recede into the background as Crisa was thinking that while Silas was writing this she had gone upstairs to change from her wedding-gown into her going-away clothes.

Nanny, who had been waiting for her exclaimed as she entered the room:

"You made a beautiful bride!"

It was then that the composure that Crisa had managed to assume during the ceremony and the luncheon that followed at last cracked.

She gave a little cry, and putting her hands to her eyes said:

"I cannot do it, Nanny...I cannot! I wish I were dead...I would drown myself...anything...rather than...go away with h-him!"

She felt Nanny's arms go around her as she said quietly:

"It's no use, dearie, as you well know. You've saved your father, and you can't let him down now."

Her words made Crisa check her tears.

"He is...horrible, Nanny...and very old," she whispered.

"I know, I know," Nanny replied. "But because you've married him, it means that your father won't starve to death. He can live here, and the people who love and trust you both will not be begging in the streets."

Crisa drew in a deep breath. She knew everything Nanny had said was true, and she must therefore fulfil her part of the bargain, painful though it might be.

She had looked very pale when she descended the stairs to find the papers had been signed and the Solicitor, her father, and her husband were once again drinking champagne.

She could still remember the look in Silas Vanderhault's eyes when he had seen her first when she came into the room.

He had raised his glass to her and said:

"My wife! My very beautiful wife, God bless her!"

He tossed the champagne down his throat as he spoke, and Crisa had gone instinctively to her father's side to slip her hand into his as if asking him to protect her.

She could feel now the reassurance she had felt when his fingers had tightened over hers.

Then she heard the Solicitor's voice, still far away, as if he spoke through a fog:

"'. . . I leave everything I possess, my houses, my land, and my money to my wife, previously Miss Crisa Royden, and on her death to go to her son, if we have one, or failing a son, any other child of the union. If there should not be one, then the money is to be divided amongst the Charities listed below.'"

For a moment there was a stunned silence.

Then the whole room seemed to vibrate with first an angry growl, which gradually increased into furious outbursts of indignation.

For a moment Crisa could hardly comprehend what she heard, or realise the enormity of it all.

Then as the Vanderhault relations were shouting at the Solicitors, arguing with each other and demanding to have the Will contested, her instinct and pride made her rise to her feet.

Without speaking to anybody, she left and ran upstairs to her special Sitting-Room which had been allotted to her by Matilda on her arrival.

It was there she wrote her letters and received any visitors whom she did not wish to entertain in the large overpowering Drawing-Room.

She shut herself in and sat down in a chair by the window, trying to think what she should do, and how she could explain to that angry mob downstairs that as far as she was concerned, they could have the money.

She made up her mind that she would just keep enough for herself to make sure she would never again be in the same position of need as she had been when she married Silas Vanderhault.

It was then a servant knocked on her door to ask her if she would receive Mr. Metcalfe, the English Solicitor who wished to speak to her.

She agreed, and when a few minutes later he appeared, the chief partner of Silas's American firm was with him.

"I am sorry if this has upset you, Mrs. Vanderhault," Mr. Metcalfe said as he joined her, "and I hope you do not mind, but I have brought with me Mr. Alfred Dougall, who as you know represents your late husband in New York."

The two men sat down on Crisa's invitation, but before they could speak she said:

"I have no wish to possess all that money, and I would like you to arrange to hand it over to my husband's relatives, leaving me just enough for my requirements, which are not large."

For a moment there was complete silence. Then Mr. Metcalfe said:

"I am afraid, Mrs. Vanderhault, that is an impossible suggestion, though I can understand your kindness and generosity in making it."

"Why is it impossible?" Crisa asked.

"Because," Mr. Dougall said in a strong accent which was a sharp contrast to the way Mr. Metcalfe spoke, "your husband appointed, quite correctly, a number of Trustees to administer a Fund, with the object of ensuring it was not frittered away or, in his own words, 'given indiscriminately to those who will undoubtedly harass my wife with requests for money.'"

"He . . . said that?" Crisa asked.

"Your husband, Mrs. Vanderhault, was only too aware that you are very much younger than he was, and while he wished to leave you wealthy when he died, he knew the penalites of being rich, and I think he also suspected that his family might be incensed at his decision not to include them in his Will."

"That is what I do not understand," Crisa objected. "Why should he have done such a thing? Why should he not have left them at least half of his fortune?"

"Because he has already amply provided for them," Mr. Dougall explained, "and he had thought for some time that they were shamelessly greedy and avaricious, and continually begging him to give him more."

He smiled before he said:

"I think you will understand, Mrs. Vanderhault, that since your husband made his money the hard way, coming as he did from a poor family, he believed that people should work for their livelihood instead of living like parasites on somebody cleverer than themselves."

"That is true," Mr. Metcalfe agreed. "Mr. Vander-hault said very much the same thing to me when I was drawing up his Will. In case you are worrying about his relatives, Mrs. Vanderhault, I can tell you that even by American standards they are all extremely well off, and your husband has found lucrative places, should they wish to take them, in his many enterprises for the husbands of his daughters, and for their children also."

Crisa thought that was reassuring. At the same time, she could still hear the angry protests voiced by the Vanderhault relatives when they heard the terms of the Will, and she was aware of how much they would resent her in the future.

"What you have to do, Mrs. Vanderhault," Mr. Metcalfe said soothingly, "is to leave everything in Mr. Dougall's hands. He and his partners spend almost their whole time on your late husband's affairs, and I assure you that things will carry on very much the same as they did in his lifetime."

"And there is no doubt," Mr. Dougall interspersed, "that your fortune will multiply, year by year."

'I must go home,' Crisa thought when they had left her. 'I have no wish to stay here being resented by them all, and at home I should find plenty to do at the Manor. Moreover, I can now afford to start new schemes on the estate for those who need work, and perhaps, because I can afford to entertain, I can make new friends.'

It was a cheering thought which sent her to bed that night happy.

It took her nearly a week to realise that it was just an illusion, just a dream that could not come true.

She had expected to come downstairs the day after the reading of the Will to face black looks and barbed innuendos if not open rudeness, because the Vander-haults resented her taking away from them that which they thought was theirs.

To her astonishment, however, she was greeted with smiles and compliments and a friendliness that had not been offered her since her arrival in America.

The house seemed to be filled day after day with not only the Vanderhaults she had met from the start, but with distant cousins and other relatives of every age who had appeared at the funeral and apparently had not returned to where they had come from.

It took Crisa a little time to understand that her wealth made her powerful and important, and, to those who were lucky, a cornucopia of all the good things they wanted.

There was always someone to ask her to patronise their favourite Charities, their friendly Church, to tell her whose birthday would occur in two days' time.

They also told her who should have a present on their Silver-Wedding day and whose child, having won a prize at School, should be rewarded with a sum of money which would enable everybody to celebrate such an auspicious occasion.

The requests were endless and while at first Crisa did exactly what was asked of her, she finally suggested that Mr. Dougall should work out what was an appropriate sum for her to subscribe to the various Charities, to finance new enterprises, and to provide her husband's grandsons with motor-cars, which were the latest fad amongst the youth of New York.

"I know that as soon as you are out of mourning you will give a Ball for Sadie, who will be seventeen next year," her husband's oldest daughter said. "We must make it the most exciting, most exotic Ball New York has ever seen!"

She went into a long description of what she envisaged, but the two words "next year" had stuck in Crisa's mind. She was thinking that she could not bear to stay on; to live in this enormous house where she had no authority and where she was overwhelmed by the Vanderhaults.

That night while she lay in bed she began to think it out seriously and realised she had been too miserable after her father's death, and too bemused after her husband's, to understand fully what had happened to her.

Now she was aware that she was a prisoner—a prisoner in a gilded cage, whose bars kept her captive and from which it seemed impossible for her to escape.

She had said to Matilda:

"I think I would like to go back to England to visit my father's grave."

The older woman had given a cry of horror.

"How can you think of such a thing when there is so much to do here. As soon as you are not in such deep mourning, there are a thousand and one duties which as dear Silas's widow you must undertake."

She had then reeled off a list of the Committees on which Crisa was expected to sit, a longer list of Charities of which she must be a patron, and a formidable number of family occasions in which she would be expected to play a leading part.

Crisa sat stunned. Not only at how much was expected of her, but that Matilda had it all worked out in her mind, making it clear that it would be impossible for her to avoid doing any of the things that were asked of her.

"I have to escape," she told herself.

But she knew, although it seemed ridiculous, that she would be obstructed in attempting to do so to the point where they would even use physical force to keep her in New York, or in what she thought of as Vanderhault territory.

There was a cousin whose estate was in California and whom it had been suggested she should visit accompanied, of course, by at least half-a-dozen Vanderhaults.

There was a ranch in Texas which they were sure would interest her, and they even suggested a trip to the Rocky Mountains, which would amuse the younger members of the family.

They could travel in Silas's private train, over his railroad, ending up in a house that stood on acres of extremely valuable land that he owned in San Francisco.

It seemed to Crisa that the whole of her life was laid out in front of her like a map, and she would be ready for the grave before she had any chance of getting away.

If it was not Matilda and Anna running her life, then it would be Silas's daughters and their husbands, who were, Crisa thought, also living on Silas's money.

They had a glint in their eye when they looked at her that told her they would do everything possible in their power to prevent her from escaping from the fold.

She felt a sense of panic sweep over her. It made her want to scream, to run away from the house and never come back. She even contemplated for one crazy moment going to the Police and asking for their protection.

Then she told herself she had to be intelligent about the situation, and in some clever way, once she got to England, she could arrange things as she pleased, and ask her father's friends to help her.

39

Strangely enough, although she had lived quietly in the country, she had been well-educated. Her mother had insisted on that, and Crisa had a good brain.

What was more, she had been given a Greek name because, as her mother had said:

"It was the Greeks who taught the civilised world to think, and that is something we must never lose."

When Crisa had been very little, she had been told why she had been given such a strange name.

"When I went to Greece with your father," her mother had said, "we went by ship to Crisa, where Apollo first sprang ashore disguised as a star at high noon.

Her mother had paused for a moment. Then she said:

"Your father was telling me the story when we were in Crisa and were looking up at the Shining Cliffs of Delphi. As he did so, I felt my baby, which was you, darling, move inside me. I knew then that you would be a very special person endowed with the spirit of Greece, and I would call you Crisa."

Crisa could hear her mother's voice, so soft and musical, telling her this, and as she had grown older, her mother had talked about Greece to her and the characteristics of the ancient Greeks.

There was especially the light that not only enriched Greece itself, but which illuminated those who were blessed with the Divine Light of the Gods.

"It is that light," her mother had said, "which you must look for and follow all your life and which I pray, my darling, you will find with the man you love and whom you will marry. Remember, it is always there to help us and if we are in difficulties or in danger, we can always call on it, and it never fails."

Standing now in the window of her Sitting-Room, Crisa felt as if her mother were talking to her and bringing her the Divine Light to show her what she should do and how she should escape.

She realised if she was to return to England the first thing she would need would be her passport.

Then she remembered it was attached to her husband's. That meant she would have to retrieve it from Mr. Krissam, and she supposed he would feel bound to inform her whole family that she was intending to leave.

She therefore thought for a long time, then, ringing the bell, she asked a servant to tell Mr. Krissam she wished to speak to him.

He came from his office immediately, and as he joined her, Crisa wondered for a moment if she should dare to be honest with him and tell him what she wished to do.

Then, as she looked at his thin lips, his sharp features, and his dark, shrewd eyes, she told herself it would be to his advantage, as well as that of the Vanderhaults, to keep her in New York and under his personal surveillance.

She therefore forced a smile to her lips as she said:

"Good afternoon, Mr. Krissam. It seems a long time since we have had a talk together."

"I hope you are better, Mrs. Vanderhault," Mr. Krissam replied. "I know what a terrible strain these past few weeks must have been."

"They have indeed," Crisa said, "and now I need your help."

"You know I am only too willing to do anything I can for you," Mr. Krissam said.

"I do not think you will find it very difficult," Crisa

replied. "I have had a letter from an English friend working here as a secretary to an author. She has been travelling about and it appears she has inadvertently mislaid her English passport, which although she has reported it to the proper authorities, has not turned up."

Crisa paused before she said:

"I feel sure, Mr. Krissam, that to help my friend you would be able to obtain a new passport for her from the British Embassy. She is worried that she will not have time herself when her employer returns to New York, and it would be very awkward if she could not travel with him, as he expects her to, on the same ship."

"Of course, Mrs. Vanderhault," Mr. Krissam said. "I quite understand, and I am certain there will be no difficulty, none at all. Through Mr. Vanderhault, I have always been on friendly terms with the British Ambassador, and I have spoken many times to him on his behalf."

"That is splendid!" Crisa exclaimed. "It would be very kind of you to arrange it, and I will write to my friend to tell her not to worry."

Mr. Krissam brought a small notepad from his pocket and said:

"Now, if I could just have a few particulars, Mrs. Vanderhault, which, of course, will be required. What is your friend's name?"

Crisa drew in her breath.

"Her name," she said, "is Miss Christina Wayne."

"And her age?"

Again there was a little hesitation before Crisa replied:

"She is twenty-three."

"And you say Miss Wayne is a secretary?"

"That is right."

Mr. Krissam thought for a moment, then he said:

"As you say, she is travelling about. I think, with your permission, I could give this house as her address in New York, and, of course, they may need an address in England."

"The Vicarage, Little Royden, Huntingdonshire," Crisa said.

Mr. Krissam put his notepad back into his pocket and after a few pleasantries left Crisa alone.

She heard the door shut behind him, and drawing in a deep breath told herself she had taken the first step— her first step to freedom.

The question was: would she be clever enough to get away without being stopped?

chapter three

REALISING it would take Mr. Krissam a few days to get the passport for "Miss Wayne," Crisa concentrated on thinking out what else she must do.

Everywhere she went, somebody went with her.

It was usually one of Silas's daughters who suggested shopping because it was something she herself enjoyed more than anything else.

But even if Crisa wished to go for a walk, it was expected that she should be accompanied if not by one of the Vanderhaults who were always willing to go with her, then by her lady's maid.

She had disliked her lady's maid as soon as she was engaged by Matilda to look after her.

She was a gaunt, middle-aged woman who Crisa was quite certain was in the pay of the Vanderhaults, so that everything she did or said was reported back to Matilda or Anna.

She could hardly prove this, but once or twice things she had said or done were known to Matilda before she herself had mentioned them to her, and she was sure the informant was her maid Abigail.

'If only Nanny were with me,' she thought over and over again, knowing that things would be very much easier if she was there.

However, she was determined that she would get home somehow, and to be with Nanny would be like being a child again with no more problems or difficulties to solve.

One of the most important things, she realised, was to have money and clothes.

The money was going to be extremely difficult, because everything she bought was put on account, and when the bills came in, she did not see them, and they were paid either by Mr. Krissam or the clerks in his office.

She therefore said to Mr. Krissam when talking about something else:

"Oh, by the way, I would like two hundred dollars with which to go shopping tomorrow."

Mr. Krissam, as she expected, looked surprised.

"You have only to put anything you purchase on account, Mrs. Vanderhault," he replied.

"I know that," Crisa answered, "but I have some presents I wish to buy, and I do not want the person who receives them to know exactly how much they cost."

She thought Mr. Krissam seemed about to argue with her, but in fact he came back ten minutes later with the $200 she had asked for in large notes.

She put them away in her purse and the next day she went shopping with Anna, who was eager to see the latest gowns, which she had been told had just arrived from Paris.

While they were in the store Crisa bought an expensive present of a blotter with gold corners, a gold pen to match it, and an ink-well, which made them all part of a set.

Although the store offered to send them, Crisa took them back with her in the carriage, and when she returned, she gave the present to Mr. Krissam with a little speech she had prepared thanking him for all his kindness to her ever since she had met him in England.

He was overcome by her generosity, and for the first time since she had known him he looked quite human as he stammered his thanks and, she thought, went a little pink in the face.

After that she asked every day for dollars with which to go shopping, buying small presents for Matilda and Anna and the smaller of Silas's grandchildren.

Everybody was delighted with anything she gave them, and she made sure that whatever she bought, some money was left over, which she hid away in a locked drawer of her desk, and always carried the key with her.

She realised she would need a great deal more than she could collect in such a small way, but at least it was a beginning, though she would have to find some means by which she could obtain a very much larger sum, enough to pay for her fare home to England.

The next thing she needed was clothes.

If she was to slip away as she intended, without anybody realising she had left, she would have to have some clothes to wear aboard ship.

It would, of course, be impossible for her to leave the house with a trunk without there being innumerable questions as to where she was going and at least one, if not more, of the Vanderhaults coming with her.

While she was considering how she could obtain new clothes, or else smuggle some of her own out without Abigail being aware of it, a new complication arose. This was that she suddenly knew perceptively that the Vanderhaults had chosen a husband for her.

It seemed incredible when Silas had been dead for such a short time, but she was quite certain that the question of her enormous fortune was continually in their minds.

They were, in fact, terrified in case being so young, she might fall in love with someone and wish to marry him.

She became aware of this fear when at a small and intimate dinner party given in her honour by one of the Vanderhaults' closest friends, who also had a house on Fifth Avenue, she met an Englishman who was staying with her host and hostess.

He was not a young man, but it was like meeting an old friend to find somebody who looked a little like her father, spoke the same language as she did, and with whom she could reminisce about Huntingdonshire, which he knew.

She was so happy to meet him and they talked so animatedly that it was only when she had to return home that she realised from the expression on Matilda's face that something was amiss.

Then on the following day there appeared to be more Vanderhaults in the house than usual.

It was quite obvious to Crisa that whatever was worrying them concerned herself, for whenever she went to a room and found them chatting in low voices with their heads together, the moment she appeared they lapsed into silence, then started up a conversation on quite trivial matters in such an artificial manner that it was obvious they were concealing something.

When two days later Thomas G. Bamburger arrived, she was quick-witted enough to understand that he had been chosen by the Vanderhaults as her future husband.

He was a distant cousin, and his mother had been a Vanderhault.

He had been employed by Silas on his Railroad and according to Matilda, who extolled his talents, he had already made a name for himself and was likely to end up as General Manager of the whole Line.

He was thirty-four years of age but looked older, and Crisa knew as soon as she saw him that he was the type of American she did not like and with whom she had little in common.

He talked a great deal, but he also sometimes lapsed into uncomfortable silences when he sat staring at her with cold eyes which told her without words that he was calculating exactly how much she was worth and how advantageous it would be for him to become her husband.

She did not ask herself how she knew all this so quickly without anything being said.

But ever since she had prayed to her mother for help to escape, she had felt the Light of Greece under which she had been born was helping and guiding her.

She was certain it was far too soon for Thomas Bamburger to say anything to her which might indicate his intentions.

At the same time, because he was always in the

house and Matilda had arranged things so that they sat next to each other at every meal, Crisa took good care never to be alone with him.

All this made her speed up her plans to escape, and deciding her next move should be to obtain clothes in which to return home, she thought out very carefully what to do.

She waited until Matilda and Anna and two of Silas's daughters had gone to a large Charity Bazaar that was taking place two blocks away.

They had invited her to go with them, but Crisa had said quietly that she felt it was too soon after her husband's death to be seen on such a public occassion.

Although they wanted to protest, they were obliged to go without her.

She waited until their carriages had left, then rang the bell and asked for a carriage for herself.

Then she went upstairs to her room, and while she was putting on one of her hats, with its floating black widow's weeds, there was a knock on the door, and as she expected, Abigail came in to tell her Mr. Krissam wanted to speak to her.

She went into the Sitting-Room next door and found him looking somewhat anxious.

"I understand, Mrs. Vanderhault, that you require a carriage. I did not realise that you were going out this afternoon."

"I did not know it myself until I opened all the letters which came this morning, and found one from my friend, Miss Wayne, whose passport you are obtaining."

She knew she was quite safe in saying this, considering that letters of condolence were still pouring in from different parts of America.

Although she suspected Mr. Krissam examined those she received, he would not, unless he steamed them open, be aware who her correspondents were.

"Miss Wayne may be coming to New York," Crisa said eagerly, as if she were looking forward to the visit, "and she has asked me to be very kind, in case she cannot stay long, to buy her a few clothes that she needs for her return to England."

"I understand," Mr. Krissam replied, "but would you not prefer to wait until tomorrow, when I am sure Mrs. Anna would like to accompany you?"

"I do not expect I shall complete all my shopping today," Crisa replied, "and of course, I will take Abigail with me."

It was something she did not wish, but she was quite certain Mr. Krissam would make a great many difficulties if she tried to go alone.

There was, however, nothing more to be said for the moment, and he went away.

Ten minutes later Crisa, accompanied by Abigail, set off for Macy's in West 14th Street.

On her arrival in the most important Department Store in New York, she sent for the Manageress of the Gown Department with an authority, although she did not realise it, that she had not had before she was married.

"I am Mrs. Silas Vanderhault," she said, "and I wish to buy some clothes for a friend of mine who will shortly be passing through New York. Unfortunately, I have very little time this afternoon, but I would be grateful if you would show me some simple gowns and, as my friend may be travelling back to England, a warm cloak which she would obviously require at sea."

The name "Vanderhault" worked wonders, and a succession of assistants brought model gowns for her to see.

Crisa explained that her friend was about the same height and size as herself.

"She told me," she said laughingly, "that as she has been travelling all over America for so long, her clothes are not only in a terrible state, but she has also lost quite a number of essential items which have to be replaced, like shoes and underclothes."

The Manageress threw up her hands and said:

"The thieving in some of the Hotels in the West is, I am told, Mrs. Vanderhault, absolutely appalling! It is something we very much deprecate and it gives our country a bad name, but what can we do about it?"

"What indeed?" Crisa sighed.

The Manageress was helpful as she ordered hats and bonnets for each gown to be worn in the daytime, and shoes were brought from another department.

She tried them on, saying as she did so that she and her friend had always been able to exchange clothes, and she did not expect that she had altered very much since she last saw her.

Finally, when she had ordered three gowns for the daytime, two simple evening gowns, and a travelling cloak of warm woollen material edged with fur, she told the Manageress to have everything packed up in a new trunk and bonnet box.

She asked her to have them ready to be collected at any time by a "Miss Christina Wayne."

"I may come myself," she said, "but if that is impossible, then Miss Wayne will identify herself to you, as I will give her a card to carry."

The Manageress said she understood and having thanked her Crisa added:

"Please have the account sent to Miss Christina Wayne care of my address."

"I hope we may provide some gowns for you, *Madame*," the Manageress said.

"I will certainly come to you as soon as I am ready to go into half-mourning," Crisa promised.

She was bowed to the door, and drove home to find that Matilda and the rest of the Vanderhault family were still at the Bazaar.

Because they had so much to talk about when they returned, they were not aware that she had left the house in their absence.

To Crisa's surprise, Mr. Krissam obviously did not tell them that she had been daring enough to do something on her own.

The following day, Mr. Krissam brought her the passport she had asked for, and when he handed her the single sheet she saw that it was signed by the British Ambassador on behalf of the Foreign Secretary.

"I am so grateful, Mr. Krissam," Crisa said. "I know Miss Wayne will thank you profusely. As I am sure you are aware, if she had had to get the passport herself, it might have meant waiting for hours at the Embassy, or perhaps calling several times before it was available."

"I am glad to have been of service, Mrs. Vanderhault," Mr. Krissam said.

Crisa knew that ever since he had received her present he had been far more affable to her than ever before.

At the same time she was taking no chances, and as she left him to go to her Sitting-Room she said:

"I will write to Miss Wayne and tell her I have the passport, but as she may have moved on from where she was last, I will keep it until her arrival. After all your trouble, it would be a great mistake to lose it."

"It would indeed," Mr. Krissam agreed.

Accordingly, Crisa wrote a letter starting "Dearest Christina" and explaining the passport was waiting for her, and also about the clothes she had asked her to buy.

She was sure the letters coming into the house were not tampered with in any way.

Those going out, however, were stamped in Mr. Krissam's office, and a post-book recorded the cost and place of destination. She suspected that anything unusual would be opened and read.

She was careful, therefore, to write nothing that might give him the slightest inkling that Christina Wayne did not actually exist.

She then addressed the envelope to a Hotel in San Francisco, the name of which she had found in a Guide Book, putting on the left-hand corner of the envelope: *"To await arrival."*

She was not sure, but she thought it would be a long time before the Reception Desk thought the addressee of the letter was overdue, and they need keep it no longer.

They would then either throw it away, or else open it and return it to the address inside.

"By that time," she told herself confidently, "I shall be home!"

The next step was to decide when and on what day she would actually leave.

It was not difficult to discover when the Liners

sailed, as the departures were listed each day in the newspapers.

Because Silas had been of so much importance, she ruled out the idea of travelling on an American Line.

Now ships could be contacted by wireless from shore, she was afraid, although it seemed absurd, that even after she had set sail it might be possible for the family to drag her back to New York.

She therefore decided that her safest way to travel was in a French Liner.

La Touraine was, she knew, slower than the German Liners, but it was beautiful and the first ship, the newspapers told her, to offer cabins *en suite*.

This innovation had of course been followed by a great number of other Liners since, but *La Touraine* sounded not only comfortable, but also from Crisa's point of view, safer than any other Line.

She would have liked to travel by one of the new Cunarders, but she was quite certain that a British ship would be the first in which the Vanderhaults would look for her, thinking she would instinctively feel safer with her own countrymen.

La Touraine was sailing to New York in two days' time, and she was aware that if she was to travel in it, she would have to choose the moment when she could escape from the family and also have enough money to pay for her fare.

That was the greatest problem of all, but once again she was unexpectedly guided and helped.

Matilda informed her that on the following Thursday she had planned that they would have luncheon outside New York with one of Silas's daughters, whose husband had just bought a house in Connecticut.

"You will enjoy the drive, Crisa," she said, "and I know you would wish to take them a house-warming present."

"But of course," Crisa agreed.

Instead of sending for Mr. Krissam, she went to his office for the first time. It was on the ground floor of the great house, and like every other room it was over-crowded.

In this case, however, it was with filing cabinets, desks, and bookcases, besides a large number of maps on the walls, which Crisa realised depicted the Vander-hault territory.

"I have to buy an expensive present," she told him, "and I think it should be something unique and origi-nal."

"You can put everything on account, Mrs. Vander-hault."

"Not at the shops I wish to patronise," Crisa an-swered. "I thought a Chinese vase or perhaps something exotic and strange from Japan."

Mr. Krissam looked indecisive and she went on:

"Mr. Bamburger was saying only the other day that Oriental salesmen make a great deal of fuss about ac-counts because they do not understand them. So give me some money, please. I have no time to argue, and actually, being English, I prefer to pay on the dot."

Mr. Krissam laughed, and taking a key from a drawer in his desk, opened a large safe that took up a lot of space on one side of the fireplace.

"What a huge safe!" Crisa exclaimed. "What can it possibly contain?"

"You would be surprised, Mrs. Vanderhault, how much money is required to keep this house running,"

Mr. Krissam answered. "There are the servants' wages, besides the tradesmen's bills, a lot of whom are paid by cash rather than by cheque."

"I do not blame them," Crisa laughed, "but it must keep you very busy."

"As you know, I have very little time to myself," Mr. Krissam replied.

He drew out a bundle of one-hundred-dollar notes as he spoke, and Crisa saw that lying beside them was a large wad of thousand-dollar notes.

She put out her hand saying:

"Thousand-dollar bills! I had no idea we had them as large as that!"

"Occasionally I use thousand-dollar notes," Mr. Krissam answered.

"One of those," Crisa remarked, "would certainly keep the average person very comfortably for a month or two."

Mr. Krissam laughed.

He took several of the one-hundred-dollar bills from the bundle and as he did so Crisa, still holding the wad of thousand-dollar notes, put up her other hand and gave her pearl necklace a sharp tug.

The pearls scattered like a shower of dewdrops all over the floor, and she gave a little cry saying:

"My pearls! Silas gave them to me on our wedding-day!"

"Do not worry, Mrs. Vanderhault," Mr. Krissam said, putting back into the safe the notes he held and going down on his knees.

The pearls had rolled in every direction, and as he was picking them up, finding some had slipped under the rugs or lodged in the wood of the parquet flooring,

Crisa managed to extract three thousand-dollar notes from the wad before she put it back into the safe.

She slipped the notes into the front of her gown, then joining Mr. Krissam on the floor she spread out her handkerchief on which they could put the pearls one by one as they found them.

When finally there appeared to be no more loose pearls, she rose to her feet, and holding out the handkerchief at the corners said as she did so:

"May I leave this with you, Mr. Krissam, to have them restrung? It was owing to my carelessness that they broke. But also, what a blessing it was it happened here and not in some public place!"

"That would indeed have been unfortunate," Mr. Krissam agreed.

He took the handkerchief and the pearls from her and put them on his desk.

Then he went back to the safe, locked it, and as Crisa turned to leave his office, he was putting the key away in his drawer.

"Thank you so much," she said. "You are always very kind and helpful, and I am very thrilled to see that you are using my present."

She looked at the ink-pot as she spoke and Mr. Krissam replied:

"I am very proud of it, Mrs. Vanderhault."

Crisa smiled at him.

Then she was running upstairs, praying he would not realise until Friday, when he paid the servants, that he was short of three thousand-dollar notes.

She went out that afternoon to buy something for Silas's granddaughters and spent, in fact, quite a lot of money, all of which she charged to account, knowing the bills would not be in for at least a week.

Then after dinner at which Thomas Bamburger was, she thought, particularly attentive, she said she must go to bed.

"I have a slight headache," she said, "and I do want to be well for tomorrow."

"Yes, of course," Matilda agreed. "At the same time, Thomas is very eager for you to see some new orchids which have just come into bloom in the Conservatory. He was saying only this afternoon before dinner how attractive they were, and I know, Crisa, you will appreciate them."

It was then the red light appeared in front of Crisa's eyes, and she knew the one thing she must not do was to go into the Conservatory alone with Thomas Bamburger.

She smiled and seemed about to acquiesce, then put her hand up to her head and said:

"I would like to see the orchids, of course, Matilda, and it is very stupid, I know, but I do feel a little giddy, and I really must lie down."

Everybody started fussing over her immediately, and she was helped up to her bedroom.

Then Abigail was sent for, and there was no further question of her going into the Conservatory with Thomas Bamburger.

Crisa went to bed after she had prayed for a long time that everything would go off exactly as she hoped.

It was not going to be easy, though it certainly was a piece of good luck that the family would have left the house to go to Connecticut.

That meant she would have time after they left to recover from the indisposition which would prevent her from going with them, and somehow to get down to the Dock in plenty of time to board *La Touraine*.

She would have been anxious in case she would not be able to get a cabin at the last minute, if she had not read in the newspapers that all the Liners were passing through a rather slack time at the moment and most of them arrived without being full, and left the same way.

She played with the idea of booking a passage in Christina's name, but that meant she would have to go to a Booking Office or to the Dock.

To do so, however, was too dangerous, because either one of the Vanderhaults or Mr. Krissam was certain to learn from the coachman who drove her where she had been, and would ask questions.

"The only risk I have to take," she told herself, "is that the ship will refuse to carry me."

In the morning everything went according to plan.

As soon as Abigail called her she sent a message to Matilda to say that she was unwell and had far too severe a headache to think of going all the way to Connecticut.

As she expected, half-an-hour later Matilda was beside her bed, commiserating with her.

"Do you think you ought to see a doctor?" she asked.

Crisa shook her head.

"No," she said, "I have had these headaches before, and it will go if I rest and do not eat very much."

"I know how disappointed Susan will be at not seeing you," Matilda said.

"Will you take her the presents I bought, and those for the children?" Crisa asked. "And please tell her I hope to come and see her new house next week. Perhaps you and I could go there together?"

"I am sure we could," Matilda agreed. "Now, you take care of yourself, Crisa. I do not like leaving you alone in the house, but I am sure the servants will look after you, and we will come back as early as possible."

"No, do not do that!" Crisa protested. "Otherwise I shall feel I am spoiling your party. I shall be quite all right. All I want to do is to sleep."

She frowned, as if it were an effort to talk, and Matilda went away after giving instructions to Abigail to take Crisa a cool drink and make sure she had something very light for luncheon.

It was after luncheon that Crisa got up and dressed herself.

She put on one of the plainest of her black gowns and carefully removed the stitches which held her long crepe veil in place on her widow's black bonnet.

Having done that, she put what jewellery she intended to take with her into her hand-bag together with all the money she had accumulated.

Only when she was ready did she ring for Abigail.

The maid came in answer to the summons and looked in astonishment to see she was dressed.

"What are you doing, Mrs. Vanderhault?" she exclaimed. "You know you should be resting!"

"I know," Crisa said, "but I have just remembered, and it was very remiss of me to have forgotten, that today is my mother's birthday, and since always in the past I have gone to Church to pray for her, I must now go to St. Patrick's Cathedral."

Abigail looked astonished.

"I had no idea, Mrs. Vanderhault, that your mother was a Roman Catholic!"

Crisa smiled.

"She was not, but as she travelled a great deal in France and other countries in Europe, she always visited the ancient, beautiful Churches.

"She told me when I was a little girl how she used to light a candle and then pray, and she believed her prayer was carried up to Heaven as long as it went on burning."

She thought Abigail, who was a staunch Nonconformist, looked sceptical and she continued:

"As I loved my mother very dearly and miss her so very much, that is what I want to do today, so kindly order the carriage and, of course, come with me."

She sensed that Abigail would have liked to argue, but instead she did as she was told, and ten minutes later they were driving towards St. Patrick's Cathedral.

When they reached the bottom of the steps which led up to the West Door, Crisa said:

"You will understand, Abigail, that I want to go into the Church alone."

"I think I ought to come with you, Mrs. Vanderhault," Abigail said stiffly.

"No, that would worry me, knowing you are an unbeliever." Crisa smiled. "I want to pray for a long time in front of my candle, which will be a very big one, so wait here for me until I return."

Before Abigail could protest any more, Crisa stepped out of the carriage and went quickly up the steps.

As she walked up the aisle, conscious as she did so of the flickering candles in front of the statues of the Saints and the Sacristy light hanging in front of the altar, she prayed fervently that her mother would help her and that Abigail would not come in search of her too quickly.

62

There was another door, which she had already ascertained was kept open on the South side of the Cathedral.

She slipped out through it and into the busy street, being fortunate enough to find a Hackney-Carriage after she had walked only a few yards.

She asked the driver to take her to Macy's and when she reached the Department Store she told him to wait outside while she hurried to the Gown Department and asked for the Manageress.

"I am afraid I am in a great hurry," she said, "because my friend has arrived and has to catch a train which leaves in three-quarters-of-an-hour for Washington. Are the things I bought ready?"

"I will get them immediately, Mrs. Vanderhault," the Manageress said, "and I do hope your friend will be pleased with them."

"I know she will be," Crisa replied, "and thank you so much for all your kindness and help."

The manageress had packed the gowns in the trunk Crisa had asked her to include in the order, and the bonnets were in two hat-boxes.

As soon as they had been piled onto the Hackney-Carriage, Crisa ordered the man to drive to the Docks as quickly as possible.

"I am travelling on the French Liner *La Touraine*," she said. "I expect you know where that ship will be."

The driver nodded and she sat back, feeling a wild excitement seep through her because she had succeeded so far in escaping from the gilded cage, the bars of which at first she had thought she could never break.

Then she remembered she had something important to do, and that was to dispose of her veil.

She pulled it off her hat, tolled it into a ball, and thrust it down behind the seat at the back of the cab, where she suspected it would not be found for some time.

Taking from her bag a mauve silk scarf which she had bought several days previously on the pretext that it would be a present for one of Silas's daughters, she tucked it neatly into the bodice of her gown, pinning it with a diamond brooch. It made her look less like a widow.

Although she did not realise it, with her fair hair and blue eyes she looked very attractive and at the same time, obviously a lady.

La Touraine, which was one of the most beautiful Liners afloat, had two funnels and three masts.

It had been, when launched, extolled as having the most exquisite lines of any ship afloat, and was called, jokingly, "the Greyhound of the Atlantic."

As Crisa went up the gangway she knew that this was her last hurdle and, if *La Touraine* refused to take her or was unexpectedly full, then she could only return ignominiously.

In that event she was sure she would never again have an opportunity of escaping from the Vanderhaults.

"Help me, Mama, please help me," she prayed anxiously as she made her way to the Purser's desk.

There was when he saw her a glint of admiration in the eyes of the middle-aged, rather good-looking Frenchman.

Crisa addressed him in her excellent Parisian French, owing this accomplishment to her mother's insistence ever since her childhood.

"I have no booking, *Monsieur,*" she said, "but I am hoping you will be kind enough to accommodate me, as I wish to leave immediately for England, having received some bad news from a member of my family."

"You are English, *Madame?*" the Purser asked.

The way he was looking at her face made it a compliment.

"Yes, I am English," Crisa replied, "and my name is Christina Wayne."

She produced her passport, which the Purser took from her and noted down the particulars it contained.

Then he said unexpectedly:

"May I ask why you are in the United States of America, *Mademoiselle?*"

Without thinking, although she thought afterwards it was unnecessary, Crisa gave the explanation she had given to Mr. Krissam.

"I have been acting as secretary to an Author who is travelling about the country. Unfortunately, as I have already told you, I have to return for family reasons and he will therefore have to manage without me."

"I am sure, *Mademoiselle,* that will be very distressing for him," the Purser remarked gallantly. "Luckily we can accommodate you in which I hope you will find a comfortable cabin."

It was only afterwards that Crisa thought perhaps it was rather strange that he had automatically assumed that she would be travelling First Class, whereas as a secretary she might more likely have been on the Second Class deck.

Perhaps he was aware of the air of opulence she had already acquired, and perhaps her looks, too, had prevented him from expecting her to travel in any other way.

65

She paid off the Hackney-Carriage, her luggage was brought aboard, and, as the Purser had promised, she was allotted a comfortable outside cabin with the new arrangement that enabled the bunk to be shut up in the daytime, so that the cabin became a Sitting-Room.

Only when Crisa had been looked after by a very attentive Steward, who had left her to unpack, telling her when she had done so he would make up her bunk for the night, did she sit down.

Then she told herself that incredibly she had done it!

She had got away, she had escaped, and unless Mr. Krissam or the Vanderhaults were clairvoyant, they could hardly imagine that she might be on one of the Liners leaving New York that night, until it would be too late to stop her.

"Thank you, Mama, thank you!" she said in her heart.

In a natural reaction to her anxiety and her fear that she would never succeed in getting away, she found the tears were running down her cheeks.

chapter four

CRISA walked around the deck the first morning after they sailed from harbour, glad of the warm cloak she had bought at Macy's.

When she went down to luncheon rather shyly, she asked the Chief Steward if she could have a table for herself, and although he suggested that she would find it more amusing to be at one of the larger tables, she insisted that she sit alone.

She not only felt rather shy, but she was also afraid, although she told herself it was ridiculous, that if she had much conversation with anybody, she might somehow give herself away so that they would suspect she was travelling under a false name.

There was no reason, of course, for anyone to be suspicious, and yet, because she had been so frightened she would not get away, she did not wish to take any chances.

She therefore ate alone, but she could, between the excellent courses of delicious food, which was far superior to anything they had eaten on the Liner going out to New York, watch the other passengers.

The French women were very smart, and although not exactly beautiful, they had a fascination and a charm which made Crisa understand why the men appeared to fawn upon them in a way she was sure no Englishman would have done.

She was uncomfortably aware that some of the younger male passengers looked at her with admiration, so fearing she might be spoken to, as soon as luncheon was over she hurried back to the safety of her cabin.

"Perhaps I am being silly," she told herself. "This might be an opportunity to meet people as I was never able to do at home, and certainly to improve my French."

At the same time, she shrank from becoming involved with the other passengers, knowing that most of them would think it very strange that she was travelling alone and perhaps in consequence the men might become overfamiliar.

"Soon I shall be back with Nanny," Crisa consoled herself, "and then I can just revert to being as I was before I married Silas Vanderhault."

She knew, however, if she was honest, that her home would never be the same without her father, and she also shrank from all she would have to do when she got there.

First she would have to talk to her Solicitors, then go over her father's Will, and finally, which she knew was inevitable, sooner or later she would have to notify the Vanderhaults that she would not be returning to America.

She was well aware that they would do everything to keep her and her fortune in their hands.

Now that she was free of Thomas Bamburger, she knew, although she had hardly dared face it when she was in New York, that she was really terrified in case she would be in some way obliged to marry him and no one would listen to any refusal on her part.

"I am free! I am free!" she told herself.

Then she wondered what she could do for the rest of the day.

The obvious thing was to read, but it had not occurred to her when she was shopping for her clothes that it might be a good idea to buy some books for Christina Wayne to read.

Then she remembered that all the Transatlantic Liners had Libraries on board, one in particular being advertised as having nine hundred books available for its passengers.

Leaving her cabin, Crisa went to the Purser's office, where she knew she could receive any information she needed.

The Purser smiled at her welcomingly.

"Bonjour, Mademoiselle," he said, "I hope you are comfortable and have everything you require."

"Yes, thank you, *Monsieur,"* Crisa replied. "What I want to ask you is where the Library is on this beautiful ship."

"I thought you would appreciate it, *Mademoiselle,"* the Purser said.

He came out of his office and took her along the deck

to where in a very elegantly furnished Writing-Room there was a large number of books protected from falling out in rough weather by being sheltered behind glass.

"Thank you very much," Crisa said.

She saw with delight that there were a number of novels by modern French authors which she had always longed to have a chance of reading.

Having selected several of them, she returned to her cabin and had just opened the pages of one of them when there was a knock on her door.

When she called: "Come in!" she was surprised to see that it was the Purser.

"Pardon, Mademoiselle, for troubling you," he said, "but I have a problem, and I wondered if you would be kind enough to help me."

"But of course I will, if I can." Crisa replied.

"We have on board an English gentleman," the Purser explained, "whom I understand has been involved in an accident which has affected his eyes. As he has some urgent correspondence to attend to, he has asked me if I can find him a secretary who will take it down at his dictation."

Crisa looked surprised and the Purser added hastily:

"I know I have no right to impose upon you in this way, but there is no one in my office who is good enough at English, even though they can speak it, to be able to write it down correctly. In any case, we are, in fact, very busy and would find it difficult to accommodate *Monsieur* Thorpe."

"Is that his name?" Crisa asked, thinking that she had not heard of him.

"Monsieur Adrian Thorpe," the Purser said slowly,

"who I understand is of some importance in England. I was told to reserve for him the best and most comfortable Suite in the whole ship."

Crisa knew that this meant that the Purser was sure he was rich, for it was unusual for a single man to take a Suite which on the Liners was intended for two people.

Her first impulse was to refuse the Purser's request because she thought she would not be an adequate secretary for anybody.

Then she remembered how often her father had asked her to write letters for him, mostly regarding horses, which he would dictate at great speed.

If she did not get it down exactly as he had dictated it, she was clever enough to improvise where necessary so that he was quite satisfied with the finished result.

"Please help me, *Mademoiselle*," the Purser said pleadingly, seeing her hesitation. "If it is too arduous a task, then I must tell *Monsieur* so, and he will have to wait until we reach England before his requirements can be met."

Crisa knew that meant eight days or more, as the French ships travelled only at twenty knots and she thought it would be selfish of her not to try to help both Mr. Thorpe and the Purser.

She gave the Frenchman a smile as she said:

"You may tell Mr. Thorpe that I will do my best to help him, but the work I have been doing before I came aboard may be very different from his requirements."

"I feel sure, *Mademoiselle*, you could not fail to please him," the Purser said. "Will you come with me now to meet *Monsieur* Thorpe?"

Reluctantly Crisa put down her novel and got to her feet.

She felt as she walked along the corridor beside the Purser that Nanny had been right when she so often said:

'One lie leads to another.'

Too late, she thought, it had been quite unnecessary for her to say to the Purser when she came aboard that she had been acting as a secretary.

But she had been so busy concentrating on her characterisation of Christina Wayne, that what she had said about her to Mr. Krissam automatically came again to her mind.

Mr. Thorpe's Suite was not far from her own cabin, and when the Purser knocked on the door of the State Room, it was opened by a small, wiry little man of middle-age, whom Crisa knew at once was a valet.

"I have brought the lady who will assist *Monsieur* Thorpe," the Purser said.

"That's good news!" the Valet replied.

She was aware that as he looked at her, his shrewd eyes sized her up immediately as a Lady, and his voice was more respectful than it had been to the Purser as he said:

"It's very kind of you, Ma'am, and the Master'll be very grateful."

With an air of relief the Purser said:

"I will leave you, *Mademoiselle*, and thank you very much indeed for being so accommodating."

He bowed politely before he walked away and Crisa moved into the State Room.

She found to her surprise that it was empty, then she remembered the Purser had said that Mr. Thorpe had had an accident.

She was not expecting, however, that he would be in bed.

Almost as if he sensed what she was thinking, the Valet said:

"If you'll sit down, Miss, I'll go and fetch the master, who I expect you've been told has had an accident and his sight's been temporarily affected. Anyway, the doctors say he's not to use his eyes, so he keeps in the dark as much as possible."

The Valet did not wait for an answer, but as he finished speaking disappeared into the cabin next door.

Crisa looked around her and thought how interesting it was to see in how much better taste this State Room was furnished than those in the American ship which had brought her and Silas to New York.

Even to think of it was to remember the profusion of flowers and fruit, the caviar and champagne with which the rooms had been stacked.

The latter had proved disastrous where Silas was concerned, for she had always been convinced that it was his excessive drinking, combined with the excitement of his wedding, that had caused him to have the stroke which had killed him.

No one had dared to say it out loud, but she was sure when she first reached New York and Silas was in a coma that his family blamed her entirely for his condition.

They thought that if he had not married her, he would doubtless still have been alive and would have returned to them as the same hard-headed business-man whose only hobby was collecting antiques.

Even to think of the voyage after she had married was to remember her unhappiness and fear of the first night, while she waited for her bridegroom to join her.

She was so deep in her thoughts that she started when the Valet's voice broke in to say:

"The Master 'opes you'll excuse him, Miss, if he stays where he is. He's comfortable there, and it'd be an effort for him to move."

"Yes, of course . . . I understand," Crisa said.

She rose from the chair and walked across the cabin and the Valet proceeded her.

There was the inevitable large, elaborate brass bedstead which was considered the last word in luxury in all the Atlantic Liners, but the decorations were very elegant, at the same time having an undeniable French air that made them, Crisa thought, particularly attractive.

Mr. Thorpe was not in bed but sitting in an armchair near a porthole over which the curtain was half-drawn to leave his face in shadow.

She saw as he looked towards her that he was wearing dark spectacles and also that a large plaster covered part of his forehead.

As she drew nearer still she was aware that he had a long velvet robe which covered one of his arms, while the other was in a sling, and the robe just rested over his shoulder like a cape.

There was a rug over his knees and, she thought, although she was not sure, that he was partially dressed.

As she walked towards him the Valet said:

"Here's Miss Wayne, who's come to 'elp you, Sir, and we're very lucky to find anyone aboard as speaks English!"

He spoke, Crisa thought, as if he felt he had to force his Master to be grateful to her, and she said quickly, before Mr. Thorpe could speak:

"I hope I will be able to help you. But also you may find me very inadequate for what you have in mind."

74

The Valet pulled up a chair for her and as she sat down Mr. Thorpe said in a deep voice:

"It is very kind of you, Miss Wayne, for, as you see, I am helpless at the moment, not only crippled, but temporarily blind. I have some letters which it is of the utmost importance should be posted immediately we dock."

"I understand," Crisa said, "and I am sure I shall be able to transcribe them for you, so long as you do not go too fast."

He did not speak and she continued:

"If I take what you say down roughly in pencil, then afterwards I can write it out neatly in ink, and read it back to you, so that you can make any corrections."

"That sounds to me excellent," Mr. Thorpe said. "Have you anything on which to write?"

"I am afraid not," Crisa replied. "I . . . I was not expecting to . . . work when I came aboard."

"Then you must forgive me for interrupting what I am sure was a holiday," Mr. Thorpe said.

He turned his head towards his Valet and added:

"Find Miss Wayne a pad on which she can write, Jenkins, and, of course, a pencil."

Jenkins went back into the next room, where there was a writing-desk, and Mr. Thorpe said to Crisa:

"I am very grateful, Miss Wayne."

"Please do not thank me," Crisa replied, "until you are quite certain I can be of some use."

"The Purser tells me you have been acting as secretary to an author," Mr. Thorpe remarked. "I wonder if I have read of his books?"

Crisa drew in her breath.

Here was another lie, and she wished she had not

said anything in the first place.

"Actually," she said after a moment's thought, "the author for whom I was working has not yet published a book but only short articles, and is therefore quite unknown. But he is now compiling a book about America, and that is why we have been travelling from place to place."

"And you found the work interesting?"

"Oh, yes, very, but I have had to return home unexpectedly for family reasons."

She paused, then Mr. Thorpe asked:

"So you are travelling alone?"

"Y-yes."

Crisa was hoping he would ask no more questions, when Jenkins came back with a folder of writing-paper headed with the name of the ship.

"I'm afraid, Miss, there's no pad," he said to Crisa, "but I've brought you a magazine to write on. I dare say you can manage."

"Yes, of course," Crisa agreed.

She took it from him, and he handed her a pencil.

The Valet adjusted the rug over Mr. Thorpe's knees, then went from the cabin, shutting the door firmly behind him.

"I am ready," Crisa said, knowing the man beside her could not see.

She thought as she looked at him that without his dark spectacles and the plaster on his forehead he might be rather good-looking.

He had a square chin, a firm mouth which she thought had a look of determination about it, and his lips turned up at the corners, as if he had a sense of humour.

It was fascinating, she thought, to be able to scrutinise a man without his being aware of it.

She felt, too, that Mr. Thorpe had well-shaped, rather elegant hands, those of a gentleman who had never done any manual work. She also thought, although she had no good grounds for thinking so, that he would be a good horseman.

She was so intent on thinking about the man opposite her that was startled when he said:

"I shall be interested to know what conclusions you have come to when you have finished inspecting me."

Her eyes widened until they almost filled her face as Crisa said a little incoherently:

"I . . . I understood you could not . . . see."

"I can distinguish only between dark and light at the moment," Mr. Thorpe explained, "but I knew perceptively what you were doing, and shall I say your vibrations, or perhaps you would prefer to say thoughts, conveyed to me what was happening."

"Are you telling me that you were . . . thought-reading?" Crisa asked.

"Not consciously," Mr. Thorpe replied, "but for some reason I cannot understand, I was aware of what you were thinking, and I know, too, that you are nervous and a little afraid, not particularly of me, but of something else."

Crisa gave a little cry.

"Stop!" she cried. "You are being uncanny, and I do not like it! If you are a professional mind-reader or a wizard, I think I will run away."

"I promise you I am neither," Mr. Thorpe replied. "It is just that when you came into the room I was very much aware of you as a person."

Crisa's fingers tightened on her pencil.

"I think," she said, "that we should get down to work."

"Very well," Mr. Thorpe agreed.

He was silent for a moment, then he began:

"'Dear Edward: I know you will be interested to hear of my journey in America...'"

He went on very, very slowly to dictate a letter that was so dull, and at the same time so unlike anything Crisa might have imagined one man would write to another, that it puzzled her.

Then as Mr. Thorpe continued to dictate page after page, mostly of descriptions of the places to which he had been and which he described in a manner so childish that Crisa longed to ask him if it was a joke.

When they had been working for quite a long time and Mr. Thorpe paused as if he were thinking, she looked up at him and realised that he was counting on his fingers.

Suddenly it struck her that the letter was in code.

She did not know why she should think such a thing, but like a flash of lightning she knew that was the reason it sounded so strange, why he spoke so slowly, and why a number of the sentences seemed disjointed and had no connection with one another.

Code!

She tried to think of what she knew about codes and who used them.

She wondered if Mr. Thorpe was in the Diplomatic Service or perhaps had something to do with Military or Naval security, which she was aware involved a Secret Service of which outsiders knew very little.

Laboriously Mr. Thorpe went on again, until the next time he paused Crisa said:

"Do you think it would be a good idea if I read back to you what you have dictated so far? Some of it seems a little odd. . . ."

"What do you mean—odd?" he interrupted sharply.

"You will find that often one sentence does not connect with the next," Crisa said, "and at times there is no continuity."

"Are you criticising my letter?" he asked, and she thought there was a note of anger in his voice.

"No, of course not," Crisa said. "I was just hoping I was doing the right thing in taking it down exactly as you dictated it."

"Yes, of course," he replied, as if he convinced himself that was her reason. "Very well, Miss Wayne, read back to me what I have dictated so that I can criticise it for myself."

Thinking she had upset him, Crisa read in her quiet, musical voice what he had dictated.

As she finished he said with a faint laugh:

"You are quite right! It does sound rather a jumble, and I suppose, because I am not used to dictating my more intimate letters, you are right in thinking it is exceedingly dull."

Crisa did not reply, and after a moment he said:

"That is what you think, is it not?"

"Y-yes," Crisa agreed.

She supposed if he could see, he would be looking at her sharply, as if he suspected she was not telling him the truth.

Then he said:

"As I am tired, I think I should wait until tomorrow before I do any more, but thank you, Miss Wayne, for your assistance. It is very kind of you."

Feeling she had displeased him and made a mistake

in not agreeing with everything he said, Crisa rose, and, going to his side, put the sheets of paper in his hand.

"I am sorry if I sounded as if I was criticising," she said in a low voice. "I have enjoyed being able to help you, and if I can do any more, please send for me."

"We have not yet finished this letter," Mr. Thorpe replied, "and I shall certainly need you to do that and several other things for me. Will you come here at eleven o'clock tomorrow morning?"

"Yes, of course," Crisa agreed.

"But not if you are enjoying yourself in other parts of the ship," Mr. Thorpe said. "Perhaps you are taking part in the various shipboard games with other young people, I expect, like yourself."

"No, I shall not be doing that."

She was surprised at the question. Then she said:

"I think the truth is that I am rather . . . shy at being alone amongst a crowd of strangers . . . which is something I have never experienced before."

As she spoke she thought that was not quite true.

She had certainly been amongst a crowd of strangers when she arrived in New York and found herself surrounded by Vanderhaults who were hostile to her because she had come home with the head of the family unconscious in a coma.

She could remember how nervous she had felt and how she had longed for one friend, one person who would understand what she was feeling.

"What happened to hurt you?" Mr. Thorpe asked quietly.

With a jerk, Crisa realised that once again he had been reading her thoughts and was aware of what she was feeling.

"I . . . I cannot . . . talk about it," she said.

"Why not?"

She would have turned away, but he said:

"Sit down, and talk to me for a moment. If you are nervous, so am I. And remember, while you can see what is going on, I am left here in the dark."

There was a plea in his voice that Crisa could not ignore.

Almost as if he ordered her to do so, she sat down again, looking at him with wide eyes, wondering how he could sense, for that must be the right word, so much about her without being able to see her.

"Tell me about yourself," Mr. Thorpe said, and now there was a beguiling note in his voice that had not been there before. "Surely it is very strange for somebody as young as you are, to be travelling without a chaperone, or somebody to look after you?"

"H-how do you know I am so . . . young?" Crisa asked.

He smiled and she thought it transformed what she could see of his face.

"Your voice is very musical and to me very attractive after the American voices which I have been listening to these past weeks. And your voice is very young, like that of someone who has not yet lived very fully."

"How . . . can you know that?" Crisa asked. "Unless of course, as I have already suggested, you are a . . . wizard."

"I have made it my job to study human beings."

"Why? Is it because you are a psychiatrist, or something like that?"

"Nothing like that," he said, "I just find the human race interesting, and I have realised you can learn a great deal from voices and from vibrations from one person to another and, of course, more especially those coming to me, and I have found it quite an interesting study."

"I am sure it can be very fascinating," Crisa agreed. "At the same time, it must be difficult for you in your present condition."

"In some ways it is easier because one concentrates more completely."

Crisa did not answer and after a moment he said:

"And now tell me about yourself."

"There is . . . nothing to tell," she said quickly.

"That is not true," he answered, "and I know, as I have already said, that you are very young, and not used to being alone, and as you are a lady, that is something you should not be."

Crisa looked at him, trying to find an answer to what he had said, but finding it impossible.

Then with a twist of his lips that made him appear cynical, Mr. Thorpe went on:

"What happened to the author with whom you were travelling? Did he find you incapable, or was he enticed away by another woman?"

For a moment Crisa could only stare at him, thinking she had not heard aright.

Then she understood what he was saying. He was insinuating that the so-called "author" was a polite euphemism for a lover with whom she had come to America.

Her whole body stiffened as she said angrily:

"What you are thinking is not true! Of course it was nothing like that! Nothing!"

Mr. Thorpe gave a little laugh. Then he said:

"My dear, I will apologise very humbly, if you will tell me the truth."

Crisa got to her feet.

"No," she said, "you have no right to pry into my private affairs, to imagine things that are not true, and make up stories about me."

She paused before she went on:

"I am going back to my cabin, and I will help you tomorrow, if you need me. But as a secretary, not as one of your studies under a microscope!"

She reached the door as she spoke, and, pulling it open, she hurried out, and as she did so she heard Mr. Thorpe laugh very softly, and it was the sound of a man who was intrigued and amused.

Without thinking, Crisa had left by the communicating door into his Sitting-Room, and when she entered it she found Jenkins sitting in one of the armchairs reading a newspaper.

He jumped to his feet as she appeared and said:

"'As the Master done enough? I meant to warn you, Miss, not to tire him."

"Mr. Thorpe says he has done enough for today," Crisa replied. "If he wants me tomorrow, I shall be available."

She did not wait to say any more, but opened the door into the corridor and hurried to her own cabin.

When she reached it, she could hardly believe that she had really heard what Mr. Thorpe had said to her.

She thought he had been insulting. At the same time, she was intrigued by the things he had said, his perception where she was concerned, and most of all by the fact that she was convinced she had been taking down a letter in code.

It flashed through her mind that he might be a criminal of some sort escaping from New York, perhaps with money he had stolen and in hiding from the Police.

Then she told herself it was very unlikely.

Whatever else he might be, she was sure Mr. Thorpe was a gentleman, and was in no way a criminal.

Again she thought as she had when she was taking down his letter that he was in some sort of secret work, and she longed to find out what it was.

Because she was so interested, almost despite herself, in Mr. Thorpe, she found it difficult to concentrate on the novel she had been reading when the Purser had interrupted her.

When she went down to dinner in the Dining Saloon, she found her thoughts not on the other guests, looking very glamorous in their evening-clothes, but on the man with dark glasses sitting alone in his lonely Suite.

After dinner there was dancing and to Crisa's embarrassment, a young Frenchman came up to her as she left the Dining Saloon and said:

"Pardon, Mademoiselle, I should be very delighted if you would dance with me."

It was so unexpected that Crisa found herself stammering as she replied:

"Th-thank you ... *Monsieur*, you are ... very kind ... but as I am ... tired ... I am going to bed."

"That is a great mistake, if I may say so," he replied. "There will be plenty of time later for you to sleep, which is a waste, may I say, of your youth and beauty."

The words sounded more flattering than they would

have done in English, and Crisa blushed, but despite his pleas she hurried back to her cabin.

Then she thought that perhaps there would have been no harm in dancing with the stranger.

But, she also knew her mother would not have approved of her doing anything so intimate with a man to whom she had not been introduced and about whom she knew nothing.

She could hear the music, very gay and beguiling, throbbing in her ears as she undressed and got into bed.

'Perhaps I ought to take my opportunities wherever they occur,' she thought.

Then she knew she was too shy to accept the sort of invitation she would be offered by a Frenchman.

What was more, it was wrong.

Crisa wondered the next morning whether Mr. Thorpe would send for her, or whether he expected her to turn up at eleven o'clock as he had directed.

Then at ten minutes to ten, Jenkins came tapping on her door to tell her she was expected at eleven.

Knowing she should have some exercise and fresh air, she hurriedly put on her cloak and went for a brisk walk round the deck.

The sea was rough, but not tempestuously so, as it had been the day before, but there were fewer people on deck, and those there were mostly men.

Some of them raised their hats as she appeared, but most of them looked at her admiringly.

Feeling shy, she hurriedly passed them, looking out at the green waves of the ocean rather than staring about to see who else was on deck.

Then she went to her cabin to tidy herself, and at

exactly eleven o'clock she knocked on the door of Mr. Thorpe's State Room.

This time when Jenkins let her in she found Mr. Thorpe was sitting with his back to the light in a comfortable armchair with flowers on the table beside him.

"Good morning, Miss Wayne," he said when she appeared. "I hope you slept well."

"Very well, thank you," Crisa answered, "and I hope you are feeling better."

"I believe I am," Mr. Thorpe replied.

Then as Crisa sat down in an armchair near him he said:

"Now, Jenkins, Miss Wayne is with me, so I insist you go out on deck and get some fresh air. After that you are to rest in your cabin."

"I'm all right, Sir," Jenkins replied.

"Those are orders, Jenkins! I know Miss Wayne will be obliging enough to sit with me until luncheontime. That gives you two hours off duty, and I am having no argument about it!"

"Very good, Sir," Jenkins said, "and if you wants anything important, you know where it is."

Crisa started at the word "important" but Mr. Thorpe did not say anything.

She had the strange feeling that he was annoyed with Jenkins for speaking in that particular way.

However, the Valet left the room, and this time Crisa had brought with her some writing-paper from her own cabin and a pencil that was also provided by the Shipping Line in a special drawer that acted both as a writing-desk and as a dressing-table.

She sat waiting, and after a moment Mr. Thorpe said:

"I was wondering during the night what was your other name."

As if he had taken her by surprise, she replied without thinking:

"Crisa."

She thought, although he could not see, that he looked at her in surprise. Then he said:

"I might have guessed there would be something Greek about you."

"You know the name Crisa?"

"Of course," Mr. Thorpe replied. "The last time I was in the little town of Crisa I imagined myself as Apollo, leaping from the dolphin-guided ship disguised as a star at high noon and marching up the steep road to slay the dragon that guarded the Shining Cliffs."

Crisa gave a little gasp.

"I have never before met anyone who knew that story. Actually my mother was in Crisa before I was born, which was why I was given such a strange name."

She thought as she spoke how the Vanderhaults had said:

"I suppose 'Crisa' is short for 'Christabel,' and it is a mistake not to use your proper name."

She had not enlightened them, but only replied:

"I have always been called Crisa, and I prefer it."

Now this strange man with his dark glasses had been to Crisa, and as her mother had done had looked up at the Shining Cliffs and known how much they meant to those who had worshipped in Delphi.

As if once again he knew what she was thinking, Mr. Thorpe went on:

"When Apollo had slain the dragon, you will remember he announced clearly to the gods that he claimed possession of all the territory he could see from where he was standing."

He smiled before he continued:

"Apollo was, amongst other things, the god of good taste and, as your mother must have told you, he had chosen the loveliest view in the whole of Greece."

"You are so lucky to have been there," Crisa said in a low voice. "I have always longed, ever since I was a child, to visit Greece, but I suppose it is something I shall never do."

As she spoke she suddenly remembered that she had actually forgotten how rich she now was.

Now, unless the Vanderhaults dragged her back to New York, she would be able to visit Greece, or anywhere else in the world that took her fancy.

Then, even as she thought of it, she knew she would be too afraid to travel alone, at least until she was very much older than she was at the moment.

"Of course you must go to Greece," Mr. Thorpe said as if he followed her thoughts. "There is no difficulty about it nowadays, and I would like to show you the place after which you are named, and take you up the winding path where over the years so many thousands of pilgrims climbed to visit the Temple of Apollo."

"It is no longer there?"

"Nero removed seven hundred statues from Delphi and sent them to Rome," Mr. Thorpe answered. "Now there is nothing but ruins, and yet there is one thing neither the Romans nor those who came after them could destroy."

"What was that?" Crisa asked.

"The Light of Greece," Mr. Thorpe said quietly.

Crisa drew in her breath.

Somehow she could hardly believe that this stranger, this man whom she could not see clearly, could speak as her mother had.

After a moment she said because she could not prevent herself:

"Tell me . . . tell me about Greece and what you saw when you were there!"

"It is difficult to know where to begin," Mr. Thorpe said with a faint smile.

Then as he spoke he put his hand up to his bandaged arm which was in a sling, and Crisa knew by the way he did so that he was in pain.

"What is it?" she asked. "Is there anything I can do?"

"I expect Jenkins is walking round the deck as I ordered him to do, and it would be difficult to find him."

"Your arm is hurting?"

"I think Jenkins must have bandaged it too tightly, and it is swelling a little."

"Please, let me look at it," Crisa offered.

Mr. Thorpe hesitated and she said:

"I have done quite a lot of bandaging at one time or another, and I promise I will not hurt you, or do anything wrong."

She remembered as she spoke that she had bandaged her father's arm when he had injured it in a fall out riding, and once when he cut his leg she had bandaged him for a month.

Mr. Thorpe, obviously in pain, finally capitulated.

"If you do not mind helping me," he said, "I think it is only a case of the bandage being too tight."

Very gently Crisa removed his robe and then the sling.

She could see the bandage round the upper part of his arm, and as she unwound it she was aware that he was right in saying it was too tight, and this was causing his arm to swell and was giving him a considerable amount of pain.

There was a wad of gauze beneath the bandage which she carefully lifted in case it was stuck to the skin and she saw that his arm was red and swollen.

She could see a wound in the flesh which was not large, but quite deep.

"What has Jenkins been putting on it?" she asked.

"Some stuff the doctor gave him," Mr. Thorpe replied. "I do not think it is any good, as the inflammation keeps returning."

"My mother always believed that inflammation of a wound like this, as long as it was clean," Crisa said, "could be cured by honey."

"Honey?" Mr. Thorpe asked in surprise. "Are you sure?"

"Absolutely! And it will take away the pain almost at once!"

"It is still hurting me most unpleasantly," he said, "but it is better now that the bandage is off."

"I would like to put some honey on it," Crisa said. "May I ring for a steward?"

"I am quite prepared to give your idea a try," Mr. Thorpe conceded, "and let us hope it is as effective and efficacious as the ambrosia of the Greek gods which conferred everlasting youth!"

Crisa smiled at him as she rang the bell and a steward came instantly.

"Will you please bring me a pot of honey?" she asked. "And if possible, I would prefer the thick clover honey."

The steward looked surprised, but he went away and Mr. Thorpe said:

"I suppose as we were talking about Greece, I should not be sceptical about natural medicine, considering the

Greeks believed that their herbs and plants, and of course their honey, were very efficacious."

"You should have remembered that before, when you were letting the doctor treat you with what Mama always said were a lot of chemicals about which no one knew, until they tried them, whether they would be good or bad for human beings."

Mr. Thorpe laughed.

"I can see, Crisa, that you have many talents besides that of being a secretary."

She noticed how he had used her Christian name and was wondering whether it was something he should not do, when the steward returned with the honey.

It was the type she had asked for, a thick clover honey and she guessed that it came from the North of France.

Opening the lid, she spread it thickly over the wound on Mr. Thorpe's arm and covered it again with the gauze. Then she bound it lightly but firmly before she replaced his arm in the sling.

"I do not think it will throb anymore," she said. "But if it does, you must take off the bandage at once. It will only hurt you excruciatingly if it is bandaged too tightly, and it will also make your arm worse than it is already."

"Thank you, Nurse!" he said mockingly. "Of course I will do exactly as you say!"

"How could you have managed to have such a terrible and unpleasant accident?"

Even as Crisa asked the question she knew the answer, and it made her draw in her breath sharply.

She was sure, absolutely sure, that the wound she had just seen on Mr. Thorpe's arm came from the thrust of a knife.

chapter five

IT was the fourth day since Crisa had boarded the ship, and she knew when she awoke in the morning that she was enjoying herself.

She found it fascinating to work with Mr. Thorpe not only because of what he dictated, which had altered considerably both in subject matter and in style in the last two days, but also because they could talk together.

She realised he was deliberately keeping her talking so that Jenkins could have some exercise and fresh air.

She had taken to being with him from eleven o'clock until luncheontime, and then again after he had had a rest, from three o'clock until sometimes as late as six in the evening.

She thought at first it was like being with her father

as they discussed various subjects, ranging all over the world.

She would sometimes argue with him, just for the sake of stimulating the conversation, and making it more exciting.

He was now in much better general health, obviously due to the fact, as Jenkins had told her, that his wound was healing rapidly.

"I thinks it was a lot of poppycock, Miss, when the Master told me how you put honey on his wound," he said, "but I 'as to admit, it's much better than anything the doctor gives him."

"Honey is a wonderful healer," Crisa replied, "and if you were sensible, you would persuade Mr. Thorpe to have some for breakfast."

Whether it was due to the honey or to the rest and relaxation on board ship, Mr. Thorpe did look better, and the plaster had been removed from his forehead.

Now she could see the nasty-looking wound that had been stitched by a doctor when he had first sustained it, and which Crisa was sure, like the wound on his arm, had been made with a knife-thrust.

She knew without even trying that it would be no use asking questions.

Yesterday, however, when they were talking after he had finished dictating, she had said:

"What took you to America in the first place? Was it something interesting?"

She knew it was a pertinent question and there was a perceptible pause while Mr. Thorpe sought for an answer.

Because she was teasing him she said after a moment:

"I wondered if perhaps, like so many Englishmen, you were looking for a rich wife."

Mr. Thorpe laughed.

"That is the last thing I would look for."

"They told me in New York," Crisa went on, "that many of the European aristocrats had travelled across the ocean for that very reason, and how the American débutante's dream is of becoming a Duchess or even a Princess!"

Mr. Thorpe laughed again. Then he said:

"The idea disgusts me! If I ever have to marry, I would certainly not want a wife who was richer than I was myself."

Just for the sake of argument, Crisa said:

"By English law, when she married you, her money becomes yours."

"That would make it even worse!" Mr. Thorpe replied. "Imagine every time I spent some of her money I knew she was thinking how extravagant I was being and perhaps grudging every cent!"

Last night after she had gone to bed, Crisa thought over what he had said, and told herself that his opinion was very likely that of every decent Englishman of whom her father and mother would have approved.

She then had the terrifying feeling that once it was known how rich she was, her position in England would be very much the same as it had been in New York, with men like Thomas Bamburger wanting to marry her, while any man whom she could love would in honour turn away from her.

"I hate my money! I hate it!" she told herself in the darkness of her cabin.

And yet she knew it had saved the Manor which had

been in the Royden family for so many centuries, and as she had known from his letters, had given her father a great deal of pleasure during the last months of his life.

Yet, almost as if somebody were saying it aloud, she could hear the question: "But what of your future?" and knew she had no answer.

Now, as she dressed, aware the sun was shining outside, that the sea was comparatively calm, and in a short while she would be working with Mr. Thorpe, she was happy.

'If only I could go on being Christina Wayne for ever,' she thought, 'then there need be no problems, no fear of being put back into a gilded cage just because I am so rich.'

She walked around the deck, feeling the sun on her face, and thought the sea looked very beautiful and that everything was so different from when she had crept aboard, terrified in case at the last moment she would be prevented from escaping.

She walked round and round the deck, acknowledging the greetings of those coming towards her with a shy little smile.

When she returned to her cabin she tidied herself before she went to Mr. Thorpe, and when she knocked on the door, it was opened as usual by Jenkins, who greeted her with a cheeky grin:

"'Mornin', Miss! You looks like a ray o' sunshine!"

Crisa was about to answer him when she realised that Mr. Thorpe was in his usual place near the porthole, his head turned in her direction, and he was smiling.

She had thought before that his smile made him look younger and more handsome, and she found herself wondering as she had so often done at night what he would look like without his dark spectacles.

She sat down in her usual chair and Mr. Thorpe said:

"Off you go, Jenkins! I doubt if the fresh air will make you look like a ray of sunshine, but it will certainly improve your constitution."

Jenkins grinned again at Crisa.

"Look after him, Miss," he ordered, and went from the cabin, closing the door rather noisily behind him.

Crisa laughed.

"Your Valet is like a character out of a book or a play," she said. "I never know what he is going to say next."

"He is invaluable to me," Mr. Thorpe replied, "and he cossets me like a Nanny, and lectures me in much the same was as my Tutors used to do!"

They both laughed, then Crisa, putting her paper neatly on her knee, asked:

"What are we going to do today?"

"I have been thinking," Mr. Thorpe said slowly, "partly because you are so efficient and so helpful, that it might be a good idea for me to write a book."

"Write a book?" Crisa echoed in astonishment.

"It was not my idea, but has been suggested to me several times in the last year by my friends, because I have been to so many strange places in the world, and seen and done things which are outside the ordinary traveller's experience."

"I wish you would tell me about the places you have visited," Crisa said somewhat wistfully. "I am sure if you described them in a book as eloquently as you have talked to me about your visits to Greece, it would be a best-seller!"

"I very much doubt that!" Mr. Thorpe laughed. "In

any case, Greece is rather different from the other places to which I have been."

They had already talked several times about Greece.

She knew he was deeply moved not only by the country, but its history and the influence the Ancient Greeks had on the civilised world.

They had talked about it as she had with her mother, and she wished now she had made notes of what Mr. Thorpe had said.

Instead of dictating as he had on other days, Mr. Thorpe, almost as if he were clearing his mind, talked of the places he might include in his book.

He spoke of India and various places in Malaya. He also described Japan, and nearer home, Turkey and North Africa.

Crisa asked questions, and he answered them with what she was aware was an inner reserve she could not penetrate.

The more he talked, the more certain she was that his visits had been secret and in some way connected with the coded letters he had dictated to her, the knife-thrust in his arm, and the wound on his forehead.

She knew there would be no use asking him directly to tell her about that part of his life.

At the same time, she was fascinated by his description of the Ganges in India, the Zen monasteries in Japan, and the strange customs of the Arabs in Africa.

Time seemed to flash by and she could hardly believe it when Jenkins returned to say that it was luncheontime.

This meant she must leave Mr. Thorpe, because she knew that being virtually blind he did not wish anybody to see him eating.

He had never so much as offered her tea while she was working with him. Now to her surprise he said:

"I think, Jenkins, because we have done a great deal of talking this morning, Miss Wayne and I should have a glass of champagne before luncheon."

"Very good, Sir," Jenkins replied. "And it'll do you good. I've always thought it's a better tonic than all that rubbish the doctors give you!"

When he had gone from the room Crisa laughed.

"He has an answer to everything!" she said.

"Many people might think him impertinent," Mr. Thorpe replied, "but his heart is in the right place, and that is more important than anything else."

"Of course it is!" Crisa agreed.

But she also thought of Nanny and how in her own way she was something like Jenkins with her tart remarks. It would be wonderful to be with her again and forget how unhappy and frightened she had been this past year.

"What is worrying you?" Mr. Thorpe asked.

The question startled Crisa.

"Worrying me?" she repeated.

"You were thinking unhappy thoughts."

"H-how do you . . . know that?"

"I can feel them vibrating towards me, and those emotions are much too strong for somebody of your age, who should be enjoying every minute of your life."

"I am enjoying it . . . at the . . . moment."

"As you have not been able to do so in the past. Tell me why."

For a moment she wanted to confide in him; to tell him how frightened she had been at marrying Silas Vanderhault, and then finding herself virtually a prisoner in his house and fearing it would be impossible ever to escape.

Then she told herself it would be indiscreet to admit that she had been deceiving him and was not the woman she pretended to be.

"I am Christina Wayne," she told herself firmly, "and that is what I intend to be for a long, long time."

Because she knew that Mr. Thorpe was waiting for an answer, she said:

"I am not unhappy at the moment, and I would like to thank you for letting me work for you. It has made all the difference to being alone on board, and having nobody to talk to."

"Talking of your working for me," Mr. Thorpe said, "you have not yet told me how much I owe you, or perhaps we could leave it and settle up at the end of the voyage."

"Y-yes . . . yes . . . of course . . . that would be much the best!" Crisa said quickly.

She wanted to say that she did not want his money and it was quite unnecessary to give her anything.

But she knew that would sound strange and he would think it extraordinary for somebody who had been a secretary to an author.

"I would like to say, Crisa," he said, "that you in your turn have made all the difference to me. I should have found it intolerable to have to sit here in the dark, day after day, with no one to talk to, except, of course, Jenkins."

He was just about to say something more, when the door opened and Jenkins came in with the champagne; since it was really cool, he must have obtained it from a refrigerator, where it was kept for Mr. Thorpe.

He poured out two glasses and, having handed one to

Crisa, he put the other into his Master's hand.

Mr. Thorpe raised his glass.

"To a very efficient, very kind person who could only have been sent to me, when I most needed her, from Mount Olympus."

The toast took Crisa by surprise.

She stared at him, wondering if he meant what he said, and expecting to see a slightly sarcastic twist to his lips, as if he were not only mocking her, but himself as well.

Then because she had learnt to read what he thought from his mouth rather than his eyes, which she could not see, she knew he was completely sincere, and she blushed before she replied:

"That is a lovely toast, and one I shall always treasure when I think of these days when in the middle of the Atlantic we are like two people on some other planet, having no contact with the world we have left behind or the world to which we are returning."

She spoke the words dreamily, and Mr. Thorpe said quietly:

"I am very grateful for this planet, as you call it, on which we find ourselves."

It flashed through Crisa's mind that her mother might think it very unconventional and improper that she should be spending so much time alone with a man, and that neither of them had anything to do with anybody else except themselves.

'We might almost be married,' Crisa thought, then blushed because it seemed an improper idea where it concerned Mr. Thorpe.

She finished her champagne and as she rose to leave Mr. Thorpe said:

"I shall expect you at three o'clock, and perhaps we

might start the first chapter of the book I have been thinking about."

"That will be very exciting!" Crisa exclaimed.

She thought about his book all the time she was having a lonely luncheon in the Dining Saloon.

At one of the large tables the passengers were noisy and many of them were laughing and joking and calling across the table to their friends.

It was obvious that all the stiffness which had made them more restrained at the beginning of the voyage had now given way to jokes between the men, and she thought the women were very much more flirtatious than they had been at first.

At the same time, they were certainly very attractive and very alluring, and she wondered if Mr. Thorpe would enjoy their company if he were not blind, and in contrast would find her rather dull and, she supposed, very English.

When luncheon was over she went back to her cabin, and putting up her feet on the bunk which had been made up into a sofa by her steward, read another of the novels she had taken from the Writing-Room.

It was an exciting story. But there were also passionate passages that made her think of the attractive Frenchwomen on board the ship, and the way they looked at the men beside them, and the way the men looked at them.

It was depressing to think that no one had ever looked at her in that way and perhaps they never would.

"One day," her mother had said to her years ago, "I hope, darling, you will find a man as wonderful as your father, who will fall in love with you, and you will know the happiness I have known ever since I have been married."

"Was Papa the only man who wanted to marry you?" Crisa asked.

Her mother smiled.

"No, I had three — no, four — proposals before I met your father, but I knew as soon as I saw him that he was the one man who mattered to me, and whom I would love all my life."

"And he felt the same about you, Mama?"

"Exactly! In fact, when he walked into the Ball-Room where I was dancing, he said to a friend who was with him:

"'That is the girl I am going to marry. I must find someone to introduce me to her.'"

'That is what I want,' Crisa thought now, 'someone who will love me just because I am me, and for no other reason.'

Then she told herself that what had happened to her mother was something that happened perhaps to one person in a million, and she would never be so lucky.

Hampered as she was with a mountain of dollars, she would never be able to believe that any man cared for her just for herself, and not because she was so rich.

It was a depressing thought, and she was watching the clock until it was three, and she could go back to Mr. Thorpe's Suite and talk to him.

As usual, she found him with Jenkins in attendance and as she sat down in her chair the Valet said:

"I'm off now, Sir. Perhaps you'll send a steward to fetch me when Miss Wayne's ready to leave."

"I will do that, Jenkins," Mr. Thorpe agreed. "Enjoy yourself!"

"If I don't, it won't be for the want of tryin'!" Jenkins said cheekily, and went from the cabin.

As if Mr. Thorpe knew that Crisa looked towards

103

him for an explanation, he said:

"Jenkins has confided in me that he has found an attractive young Frenchwoman on the Second Class deck, and he is very keen to dance with her one evening, if I can persuade you to stay with me."

Crisa's eyes widened a little, but she said quickly:

"Of course . . . I would be delighted to do that."

"It seems rather an imposition," Mr. Thorpe said, "but Jenkins refuses to leave me on my own, and I would like him to have a good time while he can."

"Yes, yes, of course," Crisa agreed.

"Well now, I have been thinking about my book."

"And so have I! You will start, I am sure, with Greece, because that country means so much to you."

"I was thinking the same thing," Mr. Thorpe said, "and also because to me you are part of Greece, it would be very appropriate."

Crisa picked up her pencil.

"I am ready," she said eagerly.

Then she made a little sound of annoyance.

"What is it?" Mr. Thorpe asked.

"I have broken the point of my pencil," she said, "and I must sharpen it."

She rose as she spoke and put her papers down on the seat of her chair.

"You will find a gold pen-knife in a drawer in the cabin next door," Mr. Thorpe said. "It is what is supposed to be the dressing-table, and I am sure Jenkins put it there beside my gold watch-chain."

"I will find it," Crisa said.

She went through the communicating door, and going to the dressing-table which had a large mirror above it she opened the drawer only to find that it was filled neatly with handkerchiefs and ties.

She looked for another drawer and found there was one in the fitted table beside the bed.

She opened it and to her surprise saw a revolver which she knew was one of the most modern and up-to-date, because her father had shown her an illustration of it in one of the newspapers.

She stared at it, thinking it confirmed what she guessed already: that Mr. Thorpe had enemies and the knife-thrust had come from one of them.

There was a drawer on the other side of the bed, but there was no gold pen-knife to be found in it.

Crisa suddenly remembered that when she had changed her novel yesterday afternoon there had been in the Writing-Room a number of pencils, besides some pens on the writing-desks.

Without bothering Mr. Thorpe, she opened the door into the passage, and leaving it ajar ran down the corridor towards the Writing-Room.

It was only a short distance from the main Suites, and she found, as she expected, two well-sharpened pencils on the first desk just inside the door.

She picked them up and ran back again, entering by the door she had left open, then shutting it quietly.

As she did so she heard the door in the Sitting-Room close and Mr. Thorpe asked:

"Is that you, Jenkins?"

There was the distinct sound of a key being turned in the lock, and then a man's voice replied:

"No, Thorpe, if that is what you call yourself now. I have at last found you alone, and I have been growing tired of waiting to do so."

"So it is you, Kermynski," Mr. Thorpe said quietly.

As he spoke he took off his dark glasses.

"Although you have been hiding yourself so competently," the man answered, "I imagine you have been expecting me to turn up sooner or later."

"I had hoped, after your last attack on me," Mr. Thorpe said quietly, "I might at least be able to reach England in peace."

"That is where you are mistaken!" the man called Kermynski replied.

He spoke fluent English, Crisa thought, listening, but with a distinct accent, and she was sure he was Russian.

She realised as he was talking that Mr. Thorpe was in danger, and she was not sure what she could do about it.

Then, as her hand went out towards the bell to summon a steward, Kermynski said:

"I intend to kill you, Thorpe, but before I do so, you will tell me the names of your men in three places which particularly concern me."

"Do you really think I would do that?" Mr. Thorpe replied, and now there was an undoubtedly mocking note in his voice.

"I think you will find it impossible not to do so," Kermynski answered, "when you receive a knife-thrust for every name you refuse to give me."

His voice deepened until it was as ferocious as that of a wild animal as he said:

"You see the knife I am holding in my hand? I shall pierce your chest with it every time you refuse to answer me, until finally, I will stab you in the heart, and you will die, as you should have died the last time we met!"

It was then that Crisa knew that it was Kermynski who had inflicted the deep wound in Mr. Thorpe's arm, and also the wound on his forehead.

She could not see what was going on, but listening,

she was sure that the Russian was standing over Mr. Thorpe menacingly, ready as he had said, to plunge the knife into his chest, then into his heart.

She drew in her breath, then moving silently on tip-toe she went to the side of the bed, and pulling open the drawer in which she had seen the revolver, took it out.

Her father had taught her to shoot several years ago when he himself had been trying out a new rifle.

The revolver was not heavy, and as she inspected it she found it was loaded with six bullets.

On tip-toe she crept to the door which communicated with the State Room and peeped through the crack.

Now she could see, as she had expected, that the man, not very tall, but thickly built, was standing beside Mr. Thorpe's chair, and as she looked she heard him say:

"I give you just three seconds to answer! What is the name of your man in Moscow?"

"I have not the slightest idea what you are talking about," Mr. Thorpe replied.

The Russian raised his arm, and as Crisa saw what he held in his hand flash in the sunshine coming through the porthole, she fired the revolver she held in her hand.

As she did so she realised what she had not noticed before, that it had a silencer affixed to it.

Instead of the explosion she waited for, there was just a "ping" as the bullet left the barrel. The man bending over Mr. Thorpe staggered, half-turned, as if to face her, and as he did so she fired again, hitting him in the chest.

He fell slowly backwards onto the floor, and as he lay sprawled there, she pushed the door open wide and ran across the room to Mr. Thorpe.

He had risen to his feet as the Russian collapsed, and Crisa threw herself against him, saying incoherently:

"I . . . I have killed him . . . I have . . . killed him!"

Mr. Thorpe supported her with his right arm, then he said quietly:

"Thank you, Crisa, for saving my life."

"H-he is . . . dead? He . . . cannot . . . hurt you?" Crisa asked, feeling she dare not look down at the Russian lying on the floor.

"He is dead," Mr. Thorpe said quickly.

As he spoke he put on his dark spectacles again and went on:

"Now, listen to me, it is important you should do exactly as I tell you. . . ."

Crisa felt very near to tears and she was trembling, but because of the way Mr. Thorpe spoke she forced herself not to cry.

"You have been very brave and very wonderful," he said, "but I cannot allow you to be mixed up in what will undoubtedly demand a great deal of explaining."

He took his arm away from her gently, in case she should fall, then sitting down again in his chair he said:

"Give me the revolver."

Without realising it, Crisa was still holding it in her hand, and although it was difficult to move because she was trembling so violently, she managed to hold it out to Mr. Thorpe, forgetting in her anxiety, that he could not see.

"First, before you leave me," he said, still in his quiet, unemotional voice, "I want you to wipe your finger-marks from it. Do you understand?"

"Y-yes."

"I have a handkerchief in my breast pocket."

She reached forward and took it. It was of white linen and smelt of Eau de Cologne.

She wiped the revolver as he had told her to do, her hands trembling so violently that she was afraid she might drop it onto the floor.

Then, knowing it was clean, she wrapped the handkerchief round the butt and put it into Mr. Thorpe's hand. As his fingers closed over it he said:

"Now, Crisa, go to your cabin and stay there. You are not to come back here until I send for you, and if anybody questions you about what has occurred, which is unlikely, you know nothing about it. Is that clear? Nothing at all!"

"I . . . I . . . understand," Crisa said, "but . . . what will you do?"

"When you have gone I will summon people to help me," Mr. Thorpe said, "and do not worry. You have disposed of my enemy for me, and I promise you I am now quite safe."

"You-you are . . . sure there are no . . . more of them?" Crisa asked fearfully.

"If there are, I can defend myself," Mr. Thorpe said, "and I assure you I am very contrite at being so careless as to leave my revolver in the other cabin instead of keeping it with me, as I should have done."

Nervously, because she was afraid of what she might see, Crisa looked down at the man lying still on the floor.

Now she could see his face, and it was obvious from his high cheek-bones that he was a Russian, but his eyes were closed.

Although she knew she had put two bullets into him and killed him, he did not look particularly horrifying, but just an ordinary, unpleasant-looking man, as he must have been when he was alive.

As if Mr. Thorpe knew what she was doing and thinking, he said:

"Now, obey me, Crisa, and do exactly what I have told you to do, and I will send for you as soon as I am able to do so."

"You . . . promise? You promise you will . . . do that?"

"I promise!"

Walking as far away from the Russian's body as she could, Crisa reached the door.

As she opened it she could not help looking back to see Mr. Thorpe sitting upright in his usual chair, the sun from the porthole illuminating his head almost as if it gave him a halo.

Then she saw the large, ugly body of the man sprawled on the floor at his feet and shuddered.

She left the State Room, and running as quickly as she could to her cabin, she locked her door and sitting down on the sofa, burst into tears.

How was it possible? How could it have happened, she asked herself, that she had deliberately killed a man when she had always told her father that she could not bear to kill anything?

She had always hated the thought of the chickens they ate being killed, or the vermin, like rats, which had to be exterminated in the stables.

'I have . . . killed a . . . man!' she thought.

Suddenly the realisation came to her that if she had not killed him, Mr. Thorpe would, in fact, now be lying dead.

The thought of him receiving a knife-thrust after the Russian had first tortured him made her heart turn over in her breast.

As it did so, she knew, unbelievable though it was, that she loved the strange man whose eyes she had never seen.

chapter six

SITTING in her cabin waiting, Crisa felt that every minute was an hour, every hour a century.

She was frantic to know what was happening. At the same time, she did not dare disobey Mr. Thorpe and leave her cabin.

She had visions of his being arrested for murder and the Captain putting him in irons, or whatever happened on board ship.

Then suddenly, striking almost like a bombshell, she realised that if there was gossip and publicity, inevitably there would be journalists.

She had an idea of how sensational the French newspapers would be if they learnt about it, and she was sure that it would be impossible to avoid one of the passengers, if not dozens of them, relating with relish to the

French Press as soon as they docked at Le Havre, what had occurred.

If there was a charge, it might be impossible for Mr. Thorpe, however much he tried, to prevent her name from appearing in the newspapers.

Granted, it would be as "Miss Christina Wayne," but she had the uncomfortable feeling that if the Vanderhaults read about it, they might want to get in touch with her to ask if she knew the whereabouts of her friend.

Everything was going round and round in her head until she felt she must run to the Suite and see what had happened to Mr. Thorpe.

The idea of his being cross-examined and, as she assumed he intended, admitting it was he who had shot the Russian was intolerable, not only because she knew it would humiliate and upset him, but also because if he was charged with murder, she would have to confess the truth.

It was then that even more frightening prospects opened up before her.

How could she possibly explain why she had concealed her identity using her supposed friend's name, or why she should wish to earn money by becoming a secretary to a stranger on board?

That in itself would seem very peculiar when she was so enormously rich, and she could see no way out of her dilemma, unless Mr. Thorpe in some magical way of his own could keep the whole thing hushed up.

"But how could he?" Crisa asked herself. "How could he hide a dead body?"

The minutes ticked by, and although she waited and waited, no one came near her.

Finally, when it was nearly eight o'clock, and she wondered if she would have to go hungry or disobey Mr. Thorpe by leaving her cabin, there came a knock on the door.

Half-an-hour earlier, because she had nothing else to do, she had changed into one of the two evening-gowns she had bought at Macy's. They were very pretty though, quite simple in style compared to the elaborate, highly decorated creations which were the fashion.

Because she was thinking what Christina Wayne, had she really existed, would wear, she had chosen gowns in the soft pastel shades that became her, and insisted on some of the frills and flowers being removed from the bodices and skirts.

Now, wearing a gown of very pale green, the colour of the leaves in Spring, she looked, although she did not realise it, like a nymph who had come up from the waves of the sea.

She hardly bothered to look in the mirror, deep in her anxiety about Mr. Thorpe.

'Supposing they have already taken him away and locked him up?' she tortured herself. 'Then I will not know where he is, and I might sit here waiting until midnight!'

She was sure, however, when she thought about it, that Jenkins would not forget her, and when at the knock she rushed to open the door, she saw him outside.

"The Master's waitin' to see you, Miss," he said.

He spoke quickly, and without waiting, as he usually did, to escort her to the door of the Suite, he walked away down the corridor and she stared after him in surprise.

Because Jenkins was behaving in so unusual a manner, it made her even more apprehensive than she was already.

Catching up the chiffon scarf which matched her gown, she hurried towards Mr. Thorpe's Suite and found unexpectedly that the door was open.

She walked into the cabin and saw that although it was not yet dark outside, the curtains were closed over the portholes, and there was one electric light which was the only illumination in the room.

As she entered, Mr. Thorpe rose from his usual chair, and she shut the door and walked towards him.

Then as her eyes went to his face she stopped still and stared.

He was not wearing his dark glasses, and as she looked at him in bewilderment she realised he was more handsome than she had thought he would be.

His eyes were dark under heavily marked eye-brows, and he was looking at her in a penetrating manner which made her feel shy.

But as if nothing mattered except that she should know the truth, she ran the few steps towards him, saying as she reached him:

"What has . . . happened? Are you . . . all right? I have been . . . terrified as to what . . . might have . . . happened to . . . you."

The words seemed to spill out of her mouth incoherently, and Mr. Thorpe took her hand in his and said quietly:

"I have a lot to tell you, Crisa, but may I say first that you are even lovelier than I thought you would be, and I am very, very grateful to you because I am alive."

"But . . . you can . . . s-see!" Crisa stammered.

"I can see because I could no longer go on without

seeing you," he answered. "So I have taken off my glasses for this evening, although I am afraid I may have to wear them for a little longer in the daytime."

"And . . . you are . . . all right?"

"I am all right."

The way he spoke, so quietly and confidently, made her aware that he was holding one of her hands in his, and that her other hand was resting involuntarily on the lapel of his evening-coat.

Blushing a little because it seemed overfamiliar, she moved a step away from him, and clasping her hands together said:

"Please . . . tell me what . . . h-happened."

"That is what I intend to do," Mr. Thorpe said, "but I feel we have a lot to celebrate, Crisa, you and I, so I have sent Jenkins for some champagne with which to do so."

"Celebrate?"

It seemed such a strange word for him to use, and she could only stare at him.

Then, as if she knew it was what he expected, she sat down in a chair which stood beside the one he always used.

He, too, sat down, before he said:

"I am sorry that I could not tell you sooner what has happened, and save you from worrying. . . ."

"Of course I have been . . . worrying," Crisa interrupted. "I . . . I thought perhaps you had been . . . arrested!"

It was difficult to say the words, and the tremor in her voice told him how frightened she had been.

It was then that the door opened and Jenkins came in carrying a bottle of champagne.

He put it down on a side-table, and opening it filled two glasses.

Crisa was silent until he had handed her one on a salver. Then she managed to thank him, even though, because everything that had happened was so strange and unexpected, she found it difficult to speak.

As Mr. Thorpe took a glass he said:

"We shall be going down to the Dining-Saloon quite soon, Jenkins, so finish up what is left of the champagne. No one deserves it more than you, but it may be politic to share it with one or two of the stewards."

"I've already thought of that, Sir," Jenkins replied, "an' I'm certain they'll not say 'no.'"

He walked towards the door and as he reached it he said:

"I 'opes you enjoys your dinner, Sir. I'm told the Chief Steward has notified the Chef how fastidious you are."

Jenkins left the State Room and Crisa stared at Mr. Thorpe in sheer astonishment.

"You are . . . going down to dinner?" she asked. "Why?"

He smiled at her and she thought, although she had already found his mouth exceedingly attractive, that when his eyes were twinkling, too, he had the most arresting face of any man she could imagine.

"Because I want you to enjoy your dinner," he said, "I am going to tell you quickly what has happened, so that you will no longer go on worrying."

Crisa drew in her breath and her fingers tightened on her glass of champagne, but she did not speak as Mr. Thorpe began:

"Before you so bravely saved my life, I thought I had

118

no chance of survival. I was in the power of a man who was wanted for murder and a dozen other crimes, both in France and America."

"But why should he . . . want to . . . kill you?" Crisa asked.

"That is a question I cannot answer fully," Mr. Thorpe replied, "but I was sent to America to find him, and when I did he managed to escape at the last moment, but not before, as you have already seen, wounding me in the arm and on my forehead."

"And . . . now that he is . . . dead," Crisa asked, "will there not be a . . . great deal of fuss? And if you say you killed him . . . there may be . . . a trial."

She shivered as she spoke, thinking how much the idea had frightened her in the long hours she had waited to hear from Mr. Thorpe.

He took a sip of the champagne before he said:

"There will be no trial!"

"N-no trial?" Crisa repeated. "But . . . surely . . . ?"

"Not so far as I am concerned, at any rate."

"I . . . I do not . . . understand!"

"It may seem rather puzzling," he said, "and although it is against my principles to talk about what has happened, I think, because you were instrumental in exterminating a rat, which Ivan Kermynski was, you are entitled to know what has happened to what is left of him."

"I . . . *must* know!" Crisa exclaimed. "You could not be so . . . cruel as to leave me in . . . ignorance, and very . . . very . . . curious?"

"And also very frightened," Mr. Thorpe finished, "which is something which I must definitely put an end to."

"How could I . . . help being afraid," Crisa asked, "when I thought you might . . . face the . . . threat of being hanged?"

"Would that upset you?"

There was a caressing note in his voice that made her look quickly away from him, feeling that what she had said had been too revealing.

"Of course I should . . . have been . . . upset," she replied, "and I . . . should have had to . . . come forward and tell them it was I who . . . fired at . . . him."

"Would you really have done that?"

"Of course . . . I would! You do not think I would let an . . . innocent man be . . . convicted . . . of murder, especially . . ."

She stopped suddenly and Mr. Thorpe said gently:

". . . especially if it was me!"

Again Crisa blushed, then he said in a different tone of voice:

"I must not tease you—I will tell you what happened. When I sent you to your cabin, I rang for a steward and when he came to the door I opened it just a crack and said:

"'Will you find my man-servant, Jenkins, as quickly as you can? I am not feeling well.'

"The steward hurried away and I locked the door until about ten minutes later, when Jenkins arrived."

Mr. Thorpe paused and smiled before he said:

"As you can imagine, Jenkins has had a great deal to say about what happened, and I could not prevent him from guessing that it was you who shot Kermynski when he threatened me, and thereby saved me from dying."

As he spoke Crisa gave a little cry.

"I have just . . . thought of . . . something . . . awful!"

"What is it?" Mr. Thorpe asked.

"It was my . . . fault that he came into your State Room as he did. I have only just . . . realised it! I heard him say it was the first time he had found you alone . . . and that was because he . . . must have seen . . . me running down the passage . . . to the Writing-Room."

She thought Mr. Thorpe looked at her in surprise and she explained:

"I could not find the pen-knife which you told me was in a drawer, although I found your revolver. Then I remembered there are always fresh pencils in the Writing Room and it took me only . . . two minutes to get one. But as the Russian must have been watching your State Room, it gave him a chance to get . . . at you . . . knowing you were . . . alone."

She drew in her breath before she said:

"I . . . I am sorry . . . desperately sorry . . . it was . . . all my fault."

Without thinking, she held out her hand almost as if she were pleading for Mr. Thorpe's forgiveness.

He took it in his, saying:

"You are not to blame yourself. It would have happened sooner or later, and how can I do anything but congratulate you on being so quick-witted and so clever as to save me?"

His fingers were strong, firm, and comforting as they held hers, and although she was trembling with the shock of suddenly realising that it was her fault that he had been exposed to danger, she managed to say:

"P-please . . . go on."

"Jenkins and I," Mr. Thorpe continued without releasing her hand, "have been in some tight spots in the past, and Jenkins knew that the one thing we did not want was to be found with the dead body of Ivan Kermynski in the cabin and to have to explain why it was in my State Room."

"B-but . . . surely it was something you . . . had to do?"

"It was Jenkins who found the key of his cabin in his pocket. This was very important since we had no idea under what name he was travelling, only knowing it would not be his own. We then rolled him up in one of the rugs."

"In one of the rugs!" Crisa exclaimed. "Why did you do that?"

"It was the way Cleopatra travelled, if you remember, when she first confronted Julius Caesar, and I dare say a number of other people have emulated her since."

There was a hint of amusement in Mr. Thorpe's voice, but Crisa could only stare at him wide-eyed.

It flashed through her mind that having taken him away rolled in the rug, Jenkins would have thrown his body into the sea.

Then she knew it would be impossible to do that in broad daylight with sailors on duty and so many people moving about the decks.

As if he knew that was what she was thinking, Mr. Thorpe said:

"No, in that way we should certainly have become implicated. Jenkins waited until he thought the corridor would be clear, then carrying Kermynski over his shoulder, completely concealed in the rug, he took him down to the lower deck."

"Surely the man was very heavy?"

"I am sure he was," Mr. Thorpe agreed, "but Jenkins was, at one time when he was in the Army, a well-known light-weight boxer, and although he does not look it, he is in his own words, 'as strong as an ox!'"

"He must be, to carry a man on his shoulder!" Crisa exclaimed.

"Jenkins took the body down to Kermynski's own cabin, laid him on the floor, with his knife in his hand, as if he had been fighting to defend himself against an assailant. Then, with what I think was exceptional cleverness, he found amongst his belongings several French and American newspapers which described some of his more recent crimes, and there were reports that so far the Police of both countries had failed to capture him."

"You mean," Crisa said, "that when he is found, the authorities on board this ship will immediately know who he really is."

"Exactly," Mr. Thorpe affirmed, "and I cannot help thinking it extremely likely that Kermynski's body will disappear during the night and he will never be heard of again."

Crisa stared at him in astonishment.

"Why should you think that will happen?"

"The answer to that is," Mr. Thorpe explained, "that owing to the intense competition among the Atlantic Liners of all three countries, France, England, and America, any scandal or anything that might lose them the confidence and the goodwill of intending passengers must take priority over everything else."

"I think I understand," Crisa said. "You mean the passengers here on *La Touraine* would be very shocked to learn there had been a murder aboard."

"Shocked and apprehensive," Mr. Thorpe said. "People think first of themselves and their own safety, and the idea that they might have been murdered in their bunks would definitely deter them from travelling by this Line again."

He smiled and went on rather sarcastically:

"If Kermynski's death was publicised, it might put off any prospective passengers from booking a passage on a French Line, thinking they would be safer on a British ship."

"Then you . . . really think," Crisa said, "that we shall not . . . hear anymore about this . . . wretched man?"

"I would be prepared to bet on it," Mr. Thorpe replied. "But also you and I are dining together tonight, which will give the assembled company something new to talk about."

"We are . . . really dining in the . . . Saloon?"

"I shall be very disappointed if you refuse to be my guest."

"I . . . I never thought . . . I never imagined that I should be able to . . . dine with you."

"You may find it a very dull experience," Mr. Thorpe remarked. "At the same time, let me say that I shall be very honoured and proud to be with the most beautiful young woman on the ship."

"You can hardly say that," Crisa exclaimed, "when you have not seen anybody else!"

"Jenkins tells me you have absolutely no rivals," Mr. Thorpe said, "and of course I am always prepared to believe Jenkins!"

Crisa laughed because she could not help it, then said:

"I . . . I cannot believe . . . all this has happened . . . it is like something out of a book . . . and even then one would . . . think it was . . . exaggerated."

"Now it is all over," Mr. Thorpe said, "and as I do not want you to think about it again, it would be best if we did not discuss it, especially on board. As far as we are concerned, nothing untoward has occurred today, except that I have not started the first chapter of my book as I should have done, and it will be something I shall do tomorrow."

Although he spoke lightly, Crisa was certain that what he said was an order and she dared not disobey him.

Mr. Thorpe lifted his glass of champagne.

"To a Greek goddess," he said, "who has stepped down from Olympus to honour me with her presence."

Crisa felt shy at the way he spoke. But she also managed to give a little laugh.

"How can I answer a toast like that," she asked, "except to say: 'Here's to your book, and may it be a huge success!'"

"I think that depends on you," Mr. Thorpe said.

He rose to his feet and she realised that although he still had his arm in a sling, beneath it he wore his evening-clothes.

"Are you quite certain that you should not wear your dark glasses?" she asked. "After all, the lights are very bright in the Saloon."

"I will let you in to a secret," Mr. Thorpe said. "I could have dispensed with them two days ago and certainly yesterday, but I had my reasons for remaining as I was."

She was certain this had something to do with his reluctance to talk about why he was pursuing the Russian criminal, and also why he was writing to somebody called "Edward" in code.

She was afraid he would think it impertinent if she questioned him, and instead she followed him across the cabin as he opened the door for her to pass through it ahead of him.

They went down to the Dining Saloon, and as Mr. Thorpe had anticipated, it caused quite a commotion when they appeared together.

A number of people sitting at the tables stopped talking to turn their heads and look at them.

Then as soon as they were seated at a table for two in a better position than that which she had occupied alone, a buzz of conversation started up which could only be about them.

Mr. Thorpe, or rather Jenkins, had obviously ordered a different dinner from what was being served to the other diners, and it was not only delicious but, Crisa knew, French cooking at its best.

There were different wines to drink with each course, and although she took only a sip of each one, she knew they were exceptional, and she was certain were kept only for very special passengers.

Crisa, sitting opposite this fascinating, handsome man, was very aware that his dark eyes were looking at her in a manner which made her feel shy.

Simultaneously, it made her heart beat in a strange way in her breast.

Though they chatted on many interesting subjects, each one seemed to concern her and become in a way personal.

She knew because he looked so distinguished and so outstanding amongst the Frenchmen that the glamorous and chic Frenchwomen were looking at him from under their eye-lashes with what was obviously an invitation in their eyes.

"He is mine ... mine!" Crisa wanted to say.

Then, as if a cold hand touched her heart, she remembered there were only three more days before the voyage came to an end and she would never see him again.

For the first time since she had thought of running away, the idea of living alone with Nanny at the Manor did not seem as attractive as it had.

It was with an effort that she forced away a question as to what would happen in the future, and concentrated on being with Mr. Thorpe at the moment.

She felt able to read his thoughts, not only by watching the movement of his mouth, but also seeing them in his eyes, as she had been unable to do in the past.

As they were finishing, a number of the diners left the Saloon to go to where there was dancing, and Mr. Thorpe said:

"Another night I am going to ask you to dance with me, but I think you have been through enough for one day, and you should go to bed and rest."

The words trembled on Crisa's lips that she did not want to leave him.

Then she told herself that would be a very forward thing to say, and if anyone should rest, it was him.

"I am sure you should not dance until your arm is completely healed," she replied, "and you are no longer wearing a sling."

"As it is my left arm which is affected," Mr. Thorpe replied, "I can hold you quite competently with my right, and I have every intention of dancing, unless, of course, you refuse me."

"You know I would not do that."

"Why not?"

It was a question she felt had an inner meaning and because once again she was shy, she looked away from him and said:

"I am sure you are right, and . . . we should have an early night."

She rose as she spoke and walked ahead of Mr. Thorpe, who followed her from the Dining Saloon.

They walked to the door of his State Room, and here Crisa paused, saying:

"I want to thank you for a most delightful dinner which was very different from when I was eating alone!"

Mr. Thorpe was unlocking the door and now, as it opened, he said:

"I have something to show you."

Crisa followed him into the State Room and he shut the door behind her.

There was still only the one light burning as it had been before she went down to dinner.

Just for a moment she thought of how earlier in the day, Kermynski's body had been lying motionless on the floor after she had shot him, with Mr. Thorpe sitting helplessly in his chair but now saved from being mutilated by the knife the criminal still held in his hand.

Then as the thoughts flashed in her mind, Mr. Thorpe came up behind her, and, putting his hands on her shoulders, turned her to face him.

"Stop thinking about it, Crisa," he said. "It is all over, and now we can think about ourselves."

She looked up at him, aware that his voice was very deep and in a way strange.

Then, as her eyes met his, she was held spellbound by the expression in them.

"As I told you earlier this evening," Mr. Thorpe said, "I am very glad to be alive, and the best way I can express my gladness is this . . ."

He pulled her against him as he spoke, and before she could realise what he meant to do, his lips came down on hers.

For a moment she could hardly believe it was happening. Then the love she had admitted to herself she had for him seemed to leap like a wave from her heart to his.

He kissed her at first gently, almost tenderly.

Then, as he felt the softness and innocence of her lips, his kiss became more insistent, more demanding.

He kissed her until Crisa felt as if they were no longer on the ship, but flying over the waves and rising into the starlit sky.

It was so perfect, so exactly what she thought a kiss would be, only more powerful, more marvellous, that she felt as if her whole body thrilled with a rapture and an ecstasy she had never known.

Only when Mr. Thorpe raised his head did she say a little incoherently:

"I . . . I thought . . . a kiss would be . . . like that . . . only it is much . . . much more . . . wonderful."

"You have never been kissed before?"

"Of course . . . not!"

"How is that possible, when you are so beautiful, so utterly and completely desirable?"

His voice was hoarse, then he was kissing her again, kissing her until Crisa thought that no one could feel disembodied as she did and no longer human, and still be alive.

Finally, because what she was feeling was almost too intense to be borne, she made an inarticulate little murmur and hid her face against Mr. Thorpe's neck.

"My darling, my sweet," he murmured, "I fell in love with your voice the moment you spoke to me, and I have been growing more and more in love with you every day."

"As I fell ... in love with your ... mouth," Crisa whispered.

He gave a little laugh before he said:

"Fate plays some very strange tricks on us. I never dreamt when I came aboard, wounded and very angry because I had not attained my objective, that I would find something I had been seeking all my life, and thought was just an impossible dream."

Crisa made a little murmur, but she did not speak, and he said:

"What I have always wanted was love, my precious one, and I might have known that the gods of Greece whom I worship would hear my prayer and sent Aphrodite to me in person."

"I ... I am not ... I would not ... aspire to be a goddess," Crisa said, "but I do love you ... although I did not know it until last night."

"I was determined not to tell you of my love," Mr. Thorpe said, "until I could see you, and you could see me."

"You are ... very handsome, but you ... make me feel ... shy."

He gave a short laugh.

"I adore you when you are shy. I had begun to think there was not a woman in the world who had not been spoiled by being complimented, flattered, and given everything they wanted."

His lips were against Crisa's forehead as he said:

"I want to wrap you in sables, cover you in diamonds, and make you forget, my precious, that you ever had to work for your living."

As he spoke, Crisa came back to reality.

Just for a moment she tried not to realise what he said.

Then she knew it was impossible to tell him that far from having to work for her living, she owned a mountain of gold which could buy her anything she wanted in the whole world.

Mr. Thorpe's arms tightened about her as he said:

"There are so many things for us to do together, my lovely one, and we will spend our honeymoon in Greece."

Crisa felt her heart turn over as he spoke, then she knew that she could not tell him the truth at this moment, and perhaps never.

Like him, she had found love, but although it might be something she could not keep, at least in the future, she would have something to remember, something to treasure.

"D-did you say our . . . honeymoon?" she questioned.

"We are going to be married," Mr. Thorpe said, "as soon as we reach England, and we are not going to wait for an engagement or any of that nonsense! I want you immediately and at once as my wife."

Because she was silent he went on:

"It may seem a shock that we should do things so quickly, but I am sure, my darling, we have known each other not for a few days on this ship, but for centuries. Perhaps we were both in Greece together, but with a dozen centuries in between then and now."

Crisa lifted her face to his as she asked:

"Do you . . . really believe . . . that?"

"Of course I believe it," he said quietly, "and there are a number of ways to prove it, the first being that when I kiss you, I know you become part of me, and nothing can divide us."

As if to demonstrate what he said, his lips were on hers and he kissed her until once again it was impossible to think of anything but the rapture he aroused within her, and she knew he felt the same.

Only when they had reached the heights of ecstasy did Mr. Thorpe say:

"Now go to bed, my darling, and it will not be long before we are together, both by day and by night, then I will be able to look after you, as you have looked after me, but I know now you are tired."

"But happy . . . so wonderfully . . . marvellously happy," Crisa murmured.

"So am I," he replied. "In fact, I did not know it was possible to feel as I do now. I have found you, my sweet, although it has taken a long search, and I will make sure I will never lose you."

He did not wait for her to reply, but kissed her until she felt as if little flames were rising within her, and she knew they had been ignited by the fire that burned on his lips.

Then, almost abruptly, he took her towards the door and said:

"Go now, my lovely one, while I can still let you. I want you, I want you unbearably! But the future is ours."

Before Crisa could say anything she found herself outside in the corridor and Mr. Thorpe's door was closed.

Then as she went slowly towards her own cabin, she felt the flames that were burning within her diminishing, and she had the feeling that the stars that shone in her eyes were fading.

"How can I . . . tell him? How can I . . . possibly tell him?" she asked herself.

As she lay in the darkness it was a question that seemed to repeat and repeat itself, until she felt despairingly there was no answer, and there never could be one.

chapter seven

FOR the next three days Crisa was happier than she had ever been in her whole life.

She awoke each morning with a feeling that something wonderful was about to happen, then waited impatiently until she could go to Adrian Thorpe's Suite.

As soon as Jenkins let her in, then left the room, she would run to where Adrian Thorpe rose from the chair in which he was habitually sitting and was waiting for her.

He would hold out his arms and she felt as if she reached a harbour of security, and she need never be afraid again.

He would kiss her until once again they were floating into the sky and the world was far away, until with an effort she would say:

"I think you . . . ought to work . . . you know how much there is to be . . . done on your book."

As she spoke she had the despairing feeling she would never see him finish it, but at least she would have learnt a great deal of what he had done, where he had been, and the strange people he had met, and they would be memories for her to cherish all her life.

He dictated slowly so that she was able to take it down without any difficulty, but not half as slowly as when he had been composing what she was sure was his coded messages to hs friend called Edward.

Sometimes she wondered if she would ask him about it, but she was sure it was something he would not talk about and would think she was intruding.

Because she was wildly in love she wanted to do everything to please him; everything that would make him love her more, and would enhance her in his eyes.

It was not difficult to do so, for he, too, was very much in love.

"How can you be so absurdly beautiful?" he asked her once.

Crisa laughed.

"You are still blind," she said. "No one has ever said that to me before."

"Then I am glad to be the first," he said, "and I promise you, my darling, that when we are married, I shall be very, very jealous, and if you so much as look at any other man, I think I should strangle you, or shut you up in a room like a Bluebeard chamber, where no one else but me could see you."

"I would not . . . mind," Crisa whispered, "as long as I could . . . see you."

Sometimes he would identify her with the Greek

goddesses he had admired all his life, and they would talk about them until, as if he were excited by her resemblance to them, he would run his finger down her small, straight nose, over her winged eye-brows, and along the clear line of her chin.

It made her feel as if little flames were touching her and because it was exciting, her lips would be ready for his.

"I love you, my little Aphrodite," he would say, "and even when we are in Greece, I do not believe we will be any happier than we are at this moment."

"When we are in Greece!"

The words seemed to repeat themselves that night when Crisa was in bed.

The only thing she dreaded were the hours passing by, and when evening came, she had to leave him.

They had an early luncheon together in his State Room, then while everybody else was in the Dining Saloon, they would walk round the deck, Adrian wearing his dark glasses because the light still hurt his eyes.

They saw very few people before they returned to what Crisa had called their Secret Planet.

Then sometimes Adrian would dictate some of his book, but more often they would sit talking, and every subject seemed to Crisa more exciting and more interesting than the last.

"Being with you is like being with an encyclopaedia," she told him.

"You flatter me!" he answered. "But I will return the compliment by saying that I have never been with a woman who is so knowledgeable or who is so interested in the same things that interest me."

This she knew was because they covered so many

subjects and she was eternally grateful to her father, who had talked to her from the time she was a small child as if she were his equal.

She had also read a great many books and she was therefore not entirely ignorant of the customs of the different lands to which Adrian had been, nor of his preoccupation with the many Ancient Religions which mankind had practised since the beginning of civilisation.

They talked of India, of the Vedas and Sanskrit, and of Yogis and Fakirs whom Adrian had met on his travels. They also discussed the theory of reincarnation and the wheel of rebirth.

Although she tried to prevent herself remembering, Crisa could hear only too clearly the note in Adrian's voice after she had asked him if he had gone to America to find a rich wife.

"The idea disgusts me!" he had replied. "If I ever have to marry, I could certainly not want a wife who is richer than I am myself."

She could recall how he had gone on to say:

"Imagine every time I spent some of her money I would know she was thinking of how extravagant I was being, and perhaps grudging me every cent!"

'That is something I would never do!' Crisa thought miserably.

But she could hear his words over and over again: "*The idea disgusts me!*" and that was what he would feel about her.

Because she could not bear to think of it, she allowed herself to live in what she knew was a Fool's Paradise, pretending that it would last for ever.

"Why should I think of the future," she asked angrily, "when it may never happen? Perhaps this ship will sink to the bottom of the ocean, and then at least I shall be with him and know that he loves me."

At other times she thought:

'Perhaps this is all a dream and I shall wake up to find I am in New York surrounded by Vanderhaults and it is only a question of time before I have to marry Thomas Bamburger.'

She therefore felt as if every kiss Adrian gave her was more precious and more exciting than the last.

"Of course I have loved you before in many lives," he said. "In this life I have searched for you, and only when I found you did I realise how lonely I had been on my own."

"Are you quite sure you have been on your own?" Crisa asked.

His eyes twinkled as he replied:

"Now you are being inquisitive, and of course there have been women in my life, many of them very beautiful. But only when I heard your voice did I know that the reason I grew bored and left them is that they were not you."

"How could you possibly fall in love with a voice?"

She knew the answer, but she wanted to hear him say it again.

"I could feel your personality, or your vibrations, whatever you like to call them, so strongly the moment you came in through the door," he replied, "and I knew at once that you were different, that something strange had happened that was so wonderful I could hardly believe it was true."

Then, as she wanted to go on asking questions, he pulled her into his arms to kiss her, and words were quite unnecessary.

Only the last night when they were at sea, and Crisa

knew that the next morning they would dock at Le Havre, did she face up to the truth that her fairy story had come to an end.

Because she could not bear to be disillusioned or hear Adrian tell her that in the circumstances he could not marry her, she had to disappear.

'I will wait until we reach London,' she thought, 'and then while he goes to his house I will say I am going to stay with a relation. That, although he will not realise it, will be the last time he will see me.'

Even to think of it was to make her feel as if her whole body were torn apart, and she wanted to cry out at the agony of it.

But it was the only thing she could do, and she thought that when she reached Little Royden Village and found Nanny she would then plan her future sensibly and without crying about it.

She knew it was important not to let Adrian have the slightest suspicion that everything was not exactly as he had assumed.

Because he was very perceptive where she was concerned and, as he had said, could read her thoughts, she knew how careful she must be in case he guessed that she intended to leave him.

During the last two days his arm had been so much better that he had discarded his sling, and Crisa knew from Jenkins that the wound was practically healed.

"It is the honey that has done it!" she exclaimed delightedly.

"If you're not careful, Miss, you'll get yourself burnt as a witch!" Jenkins said. "But I 'as to admit the Master's better and happier than I've ever known him!"

He grinned at her as he spoke, and Crisa knew he

140

was well aware of what they felt for each other.

When she awoke to see the coast of France from her porthole, she had a wild impulse to run to Adrian and tell him the truth.

"He loves me . . . he loves me enough," she said in her heart defiantly.

Then once again she could hear him saying that the idea of a rich wife disgusted him, and she knew that her mountain of gold would be a stumbling block for any man, let alone somebody as positive in his views as Adrian.

"I love him! I love him!" Crisa said despairingly, but she knew that to cope with this obstacle, love was not enough.

She had packed her luggage the night before, and now when it was ready and labelled for London she went from her cabin, carrying her cloak over her arm, towards Adrian's State Room.

Jenkins let her in.

" 'Mornin', Miss!" he said cheerfully. "The Master's nearly ready!"

"Come here, Crisa!" he heard Adrian call from the other cabin.

She went in through the communicating door to find him already dressed.

He was not wearing his dark glasses and she thought as she looked at him how extremely handsome he was and how different from any man she had ever seen.

He smiled at her and said:

"When Jenkins was packing he came across a photograph of my house which I took with the first camera I ever owned. I thought you might like to see it."

"Of course I would!" Crisa cried.

He turned to Jenkins.

"Fetch Miss Wayne's luggage and put it with mine, then it can go directly into our cabin on the steamer."

"Yes, of course, Sir," Jenkins said, and left.

Then Adrian said:

"Before I show you anything, I want to tell you how lovely you are looking this morning, and I also want to kiss you."

Crisa raised her face to his.

"That is . . . what I want . . . too," he whispered.

He put his arms around her, and his lips had just touched hers when the door opened and Jenkins came back into the cabin.

Instinctively they moved apart as he said in a low voice:

"There's two officers from the *Sûreté*, Sir, to see you."

Crisa gave a little gasp and Adrian stiffened. Then he asked:

"They are in the State Room next door?"

"Yes, Sir."

"Very well, I will see them. You fetch the luggage, as I told you."

Jenkins went out into the corridor and Adrian moved towards the communicating door.

"Wait here!" he said very softly to Crisa, and disappeared into the State Room.

Crisa waited, her heart pounding.

Then she realised that although Adrian had closed the door behind him, it was not latched securely.

She could therefore hear him say quite distinctly in his excellent French:

"Good-morning, gentlemen, what can I do for you?"

"You are Milord Hawthorpe?" one of the officers enquired.

"I am!"

"Then we are honoured to meet you, *Monsieur*, and we have been instructed by the *Chef de la Sûreté* in Paris to convey to you his compliments and to ask if you would be kind enough to accept his invitation, together with that of the Prime Minister, to go immediately to Paris, instead of returning, as we understand you intend to do, to England."

There was a short pause while Crisa, listening, could hardly believe what she was hearing.

How was it possible that the man she had known and loved as Adrian Thorpe was in fact a member of the aristocracy and someone, she was quite sure, who was very important?

"Why did you not tell me?" she longed to ask him, but could only listen as he replied:

"You say the Prime Minister wishes to see me?"

"It is not only the Prime Minister, Milord," was the reply, "but also *Le Président* himself. In fact, he has already arranged for the Presidential Coach to be attached to the train, so that you may travel in comfort."

There was a note of awe in the speaker's voice which told Crisa what this privilege meant.

She was not surprised to hear Adrian answer:

"In that case, *Messieurs*, you will understand I should be honoured to accept both your President and your Prime Minister's invitation, and I will, at their request, change my plans and proceed to Paris."

"*Merci, Monsieur*, we are very grateful."

"I am sure it is not too early in the morning," Crisa heard Adrian add, "to offer you a drink. Will you have a glass of sherry, or would you prefer something else?"

Crisa knew he had walked across the cabin to where on a sideboard there were a number of different bottles and glasses, that had been there all during the voyage.

It was when she heard the two men from the *Sûreté* mumble acceptance that she realised her luggage must not be put in the train with Adrian's, but should travel with her in the Steamer that was waiting to convey the English passengers to Southampton.

Opening the door into the corridor, she planned to find Jenkins and prevent him from moving her luggage as his Master had told him to do.

To reach her own cabin she had to pass the Purser's office, which stood at the top of the stairs leading down to the Dining Saloon.

There were a great number of people, most of them intent on leaving the ship for the train to Paris, and just a few English travellers who were to cross the Channel.

Crisa was hurrying on to her own cabin when she heard a man speaking in a distinctly English voice which seemed to ring out clearly above the chatter of French voices.

". . . I wish to speak immediately, before she leaves the ship, to Miss Christina Wayne!"

She was so surprised at what she heard that she stopped dead, looked towards the Purser's office, and saw standing at the open desk a tall man with his back to her.

She could not see his face, but she knew immediately that it was Mr. Metcalfe, her late husband's solicitor in England!

It was then with a sense of panic, without thinking, that she ran back along the corridor from which she had just come, not stopping at the familiar State Room, where she had been so happy, but on to the very end, where she knew there was a stairway leading down to the lower deck.

As she reached the Second Class she sped along the corridor pushing past a number of people with their luggage, until she found the gang-plank that led her onto the Quay.

Still pushing and shoving her way past men carrying cases, women with bundles and babies, she reached the Quay, and found her way to the Channel Steamer.

Fortunately when she had boarded *La Touraine* she had also explained she was going to England and had bought a ticket which entitled her to be a First Class passenger on a Steamer to Southampton.

As soon as she was on board she went down into the Saloon and seated herself in the most obscure corner she could find.

There were a number of elderly men and women already there, but she fancied those who were younger and more adventurous would prefer to be on deck.

She was, however, concerned with nothing except escaping from Mr. Metcalfe.

She realised now that he must have been informed by wireless from America that she was missing, and perhaps either he or members of his staff had met every Liner that had left New York on the day she had disappeared into St. Patrick's Cathedral.

She felt she should commend the Vanderhaults for their efficiency, but at the same time she was terrified.

She was sure she would be brow-beaten and somehow coerced into returning back to Silas's relatives, who would all be waiting for her and with them Thomas Bamburger.

She suspected, however, that Mr. Metcalfe was genuinely looking for "Christina Wayne" but the moment he saw her he would recognise her and the search would be over.

"He cannot make me go back," Crisa told herself.

But she knew that with no one to support her it would be almost impossible to hold out against the will and determination of the whole Vanderhault family and their legal advisors like Mr. Metcalfe, who would all be on their side.

Once again she was alone, but she thought frantically that if she could just reach England, there would be somewhere she would hide where they would not find her.

She wanted to think. She could not bear to look at the people around her, or hear the chatter and noise as they talked and laughed.

She put her hands up to her face, trying to plan, at the same time praying with an urgency that seemed to come from the very depths of her soul that she could escape.

"Oh, God, help me!" she prayed.

Then she almost gave a little scream as she felt somebody touch her shoulder lightly.

She looked up, afraid of whom she might see, and saw it was Jenkins.

"The Master wants you, Miss," he said simply.

"I . . . I cannot . . . I have to . . . go . . ."

Suddenly the words died on her lips.

It was no use.

If Adrian wanted her, there was nothing she could do but go to him, even if it meant he was handing her over to Mr. Metcalfe.

Jenkins was waiting and, although she wanted to

argue, it was impossible to do so because he was only carrying out his Master's orders and they were surrounded by people staring at them curiously.

She got to her feet, aware as she did so that apart from looking much smarter and more elegant than anyone else, she had left her fur-trimmed cape behind and she would, if she had sailed without it, have found it very cold at sea.

This was a problem that no longer arose, and she followed Jenkins off the streamer and onto the dock, feeling not unlike a child who has misbehaved by running away from her Nurse or her teacher.

On the other hand, she was also a prisoner being taken back into a cage which there would be no escape.

Now as she stood in the sunshine she wondered if she should insist on travelling to England as she had intended.

Then she knew she had not the courage to defy Adrian, who had sent for her, and anyway by this time Mr. Metcalfe would have described her to him and he would know who she was. . . .

"You'll have to hurry, Miss," Jenkins said, breaking in on her thoughts, "they're 'olding the train until you gets there."

"The . . . the train?" Crisa gasped.

Then it was impossible to talk as Jenkins, who was walking so quickly that she almost had to run to keep up, was leading her away from the Quay, where she had boarded the Steamer, and to the other side of the dock, where the train for Paris was drawn up alongside *La Touraine*.

As they reached it she was aware of several *gendarmes* and two men in uniform who looked, she thought, as if they were members of the *Sûreté* waiting beside one of the coaches which was attached to the end of the train, and painted a different colour, looked very impressive.

Then Jenkins was guiding her up the steps and into what Crisa saw was a Drawing-Room compartment.

Standing in the centre of it, very tall, important and, she thought somehow frightening, was Adrian.

For a moment they just looked at each other, and as her eyes seemed to fill her whole face he realised how nervous and upset she was.

He did not speak to her, instead he said to the man standing just inside the door:

"Now that Miss Wayne has joined me, *Monsieur*, the train can depart, and I can only express my regret at the delay."

"*Merci*, Milord," the Frenchman said. "*Bon voyage!*"

He left the compartment and Jenkins followed him.

There was the chatter of voices and a shrill whistle as the guard signalled the departure of the train and a second later it started to move.

"Come to sit down," Adrian said.

He put out his hand as he spoke to steady her as the train started moving.

Then as she sank down on the nearest seat, which happened to be a sofa on which he could sit beside her, he asked, still in the same quiet voice:

"Why did you not tell me?"

"H-how could I . . . ?" Crisa began, then she asked: "What has . . . happened? You know I cannot . . . come with you . . . and where is . . . Mr. Metcalfe?"

Adrian smiled before he replied:

"So many questions, when I think I should be the one asking them."

"N-no . . . you have . . . no right."

"I thought I had every right, seeing that I am going to be your husband."

Crisa drew in a deep breath before she said:

"I . . . I thought you . . . must have seen . . . Mr. Metcalfe."

"I have seen him, and he told me he wished to question a Miss Christina Wayne about the disappearance of Mrs. Crisa Vanderhault from New York on the same day as she embarked on *La Touraine*."

Crisa closed her eyes, but she did not speak.

Then Adrian said:

"I could hardly believe there was another woman as beautiful as Mr. Metcalfe described to me, who was also called 'Crisa.' "

"So now you know . . . or rather . . . you have . . . guessed."

Crisa spoke with a note of panic in her voice as she added:

"But where . . . is Mr. Metcalfe? What have you . . . done with . . . him? Is he waiting for me . . . somewhere on the . . . train?"

"I assured him that with the help of Miss Christina Wayne I will let him know the whereabouts of Mrs. Crisa Vanderhault very shortly."

"You . . . told him . . . that?"

"Yes, and he was quite satisfied. I left him enjoying a glass of champagne in my State Room while I boarded the train."

"Then he has . . . no idea that I am . . . with you?"

"Not unless he is a thought-reader."

Crisa gave a deep sigh of relief. She felt as if it were possible to breathe again and the blood came back into her heart.

"That means I have a chance to escape," she said. "Oh, please . . . please . . . help me to hide where they cannot find me . . . and make me go back to . . . New York."

"That is not difficult."

"You do not . . . understand . . . it is very difficult . . . there are so many of them . . . they are . . . overwhelming, and they are . . . determined to prevent me from going away from them . . . that is why I . . . invented Christina Wayne!"

"That was very intelligent of you, and you must tell me all about it," Adrian said. "In the meantime, I cannot have you looking as frightened as you do now, when there is no need for it."

"That is because you do not . . . understand," Crisa cried. "I have to hide . . . and of course it is . . . frightening!"

"I agree you have to hide," Adrian said, "and I am prepared to help you."

"Will you really . . . will you really . . . help me?"

"Of course! And that is why we will be married the moment we reach Paris."

There was a sudden silence while Crisa looked at him as if she could not believe what he had said.

Then slowly, hesitatingly, as if it were hard to speak, she said:

"Y-you know that I . . . cannot marry you."

"Why not?"

"Because . . . of my m-money . . . I know what you feel about . . . women with money . . . and I have so much . . . and they will not . . . let me give it . . . away."

"When I spoke about women with money," Adrian replied, "I was speaking in the abstract, while now I am speaking about you."

150

"Do you think I could marry you," Crisa asked, "knowing that you said the idea ... disgusted you ... and you would never have a wife who was richer than you are yourself?"

"That is what I still feel in principle," he said, "but actually, my darling, I would marry you if you had not a penny to your name, which I believed, since you were working as a secretary, or on the contrary if you were as rich as Croesus or even if you had a mountain of gold!"

"That is ... exactly what I do ... have," Crisa said with a little sob in her voice.

"Then one way or another we will put it to some sensible use," Adrian said. "I have every intention of making you my wife and I will not be diverted from that object by anything you may possess or not possess."

"You ... do not mean that ... because you do not ... understand!"

He laughed and it was, she thought, a very happy sound.

Then he bent forward, and to her surprise undid the ribbons of her bonnet, which she had tied under her chin, and taking if off, he threw it onto the floor.

He put his arms around her and drew her close against him, saying:

"I cannot think why we are arguing about something which is not of the least importance, when I might be kissing you."

He did not wait for her reply, but his lips were on hers.

He kissed her possessively, passionately, demandingly, until it was impossible to think, impossible to know anything but the sense of rapture and ecstasy he always evoked in her.

She felt thrills like little shafts of lightning running

through her, and her whole body wanted to melt into his.

Because she had been so frightened, because she had thought she was going to be taken back into captivity by Mr. Metcalfe, and mostly because she had thought she would have to lose him, the tears ran down her cheeks even while her whole being pulsated with the wonder of his kisses.

He raised her face up to his, then, seeing her tears, wiped them away very gently.

"There is nothing to cry about, my darling," he said softly.

"I . . . I thought . . . as you could not . . . love me . . . that I would never . . . see you again."

"Do you really think I could lose you?" he asked. "How dare you doubt my love!"

"I . . . I could not believe . . . after all you said . . . that when you knew the truth about me . . . you would go on . . . loving me."

"Now you know that nothing matters in my life but you, and nothing else ever will."

He kissed her again, then as she put her head on his shoulder she said:

"Those men called you 'Lord Hawthorpe!' Why did you . . . not tell me who you were?"

"I was travelling, as you very likely understand by this time, on a very delicate mission, and also a very dangerous one. I had to leave America in a hurry because I had been wounded, and when as Kermynski had disappeared I thought I would do no good by staying, especially as I could not see."

Crisa made a little sound of horror.

"Instead of having a false passport made," he went

152

on, "and anyway there was no time for that—I used the one I had before I came into my father's title, and hoped that Kermynski, who was a very unpleasant and dangerous man, would not be able to find me."

"But he did!"

"But thanks to you, my darling, he will not trouble me or anybody else in the future."

Crisa gave a cry.

"I have been so selfish . . . thinking about . . . myself," she said, "that I have not . . . worried about you. There is not going to be any . . . trouble in Paris?"

"Not trouble, but a great many congratulations," Adrian said. "It is you who should be the one to receive them, not me!"

"No, of course not! You know I would not want . . . anybody to know I was . . . involved."

"As my wife," Adrian said, "you will not be involved in anything of this sort again, nor in the future will I."

His arms tightened around her as he said:

"I am afraid, my precious, you may find it very dull living in the country and looking after the people who have been employed on my estate for generations, and of course opening the Flower Show, and being a very important lady in the County."

The way he spoke, with a mocking note in his voice, made Crisa give a little watery laugh before she said:

"You know all I . . . want is to be . . . with you."

"As you will be," Adrian said. "But first, my lovely one, we will be married and have the honeymoon I promised you in Greece before we take up our duties in England."

Crisa looked at him enquiringly, and he said:

153

"Do not worry about what will happen in Paris. I suspect secretly and behind closed doors I shall have to tell *Monsieur* Jules Méline, the Prime Minister, how I disposed of Kermynski, but no one else will ever know exactly what occurred."

"There is . . . no question of your having to stand . . . trial?" Crisa asked in a low voice.

"None at all," Adrian replied. "Kermynski's body was secretly committed to the ocean without anybody being aware of it the night after it was found in his cabin, and if his confederates in various parts of the world are waiting for him, they will wait in vain!"

"And no one . . . else will . . . threaten you?"

"I was not threatened in the first place," Adrian answered. "The man who was threatened was the President of France, *Monsieur* Félix Faure, and Kermynski very nearly managed to murder him. However, he failed, and when the *Sûreté* very foolishly let him escape, he fled to America.

"It was then, because I have been successful in the same sort of situation in the past, that they asked me to find Kermynski and make sure he could not attack the President, or anyone else of equal importance again."

He smiled as he said:

"As you know, I failed, but a very lovely young woman posing as my secretary succeeded, and I am only sorry that I cannot tell the world how clever as well as beautiful she is."

"No, no!" Crisa begged. "I could not . . . bear it! I do not want anyone to know . . . where I am, or . . . who I am."

"All the world is going to know that I am married to a very beautiful woman," Adrian said. "She is English, and comes from a very old and respected English family."

Crisa looked at him in surprise.

"H-how did you know that?"

"Mr. Metcalfe told me that your father was the late Sir Robert Royden, and in fact I knew him."

"You knew Papa?"

"I met him several times at Tattersall's when I was selling or buying horses, and I thought he was not only charming, but very knowledgeable. I might have guessed that his daughter would be exactly the same."

"I know nothing except about living in the country and leading a very quite life," Crisa said.

She moved a little closer to him as she said:

"I am frightened that I shall . . . bore you . . . and you will find me very dull and . . . ignorant."

"At the moment," Adrian said, "I find you very exciting, very intelligent, and very innocent; qualities, my beautiful little goddess, which enthral and captivate me and which I feel will keep me enchanted for the next thousand years!"

Crisa laughed, but she was very near to tears as she said:

"Is it true . . . really true that I can marry you, and you really do not mind that I m-married Silas Vanderhault? It was the . . . only way I could . . . save Papa from being bankrupted and perhaps sent to prison."

"I guessed that might be the reason," Adrian said quietly. "Mr. Metcalfe told me how your husband collapsed on your wedding-night, and I knew when I kissed you that you had never been kissed before."

"How can you be so wonderful?" Crisa asked. "But there is . . . still that money . . . which they will . . . not let me . . . give away."

"Mr. Metcalfe also told me that you tried to do so, but I feel that together we can think of ways of disposing of it, or rather, preventing it from troubling us in the future."

"H-how can we do that?" Crisa asked. "The Vanderhaults are quite fanatical when it comes to money, and they wanted me to . . . marry a horrible man called Thomas Bamburger, who is the Managing Director of their Railway, just so that I could never . . . escape from them, and from the . . . millions of dollars that Silas left me."

"They will have no hold over you once you are married to me," Adrian said firmly, "and what I am already planning is that we will create various Trusts, my darling, which cannot be rejected, as your offer was, by the Vanderhaults' Trustees, because they will be for the good of the community."

"Do you really mean that?" Crisa asked.

"As I cannot have a wife with so many dollars attached to her," Adrian smiled, "I have every intention of setting up on your behalf a Trust for the development of new inventions and new ideas. I think, too, we could have a Trust for the Arts, and another for destitute children, besides various other Charities, who invariably need millions of dollars a year, and never have enough."

He laughed as he added:

"In fact, darling, you will soon find that you have to rely on your husband for every gown you buy and for every pair of shoes you wish to put on your tiny feet."

"That is exactly what I want," Crisa cried. "I want not only to rely on you, but to be with you and love you . . . and have nothing and nobody interfering."

"I will make certain of that."

Then Adrian was kissing her again, kissing her with a determination and a passion which told Crisa she need no longer be afraid, no longer feel she was caught in a golden cage from which there was no escape.

"I love you! I love you! I love you!" the wheels of the train were saying beneath them, all the way to Paris.

Lord and Lady Hawthorpe left Paris two days later, after their marriage had taken place before the Mayor, as was compulsory in France, following which they had a quiet ceremony in the British Embassy Church.

"There are a great many things, my beautiful, adorable wife, that I want to show you in Paris," Adrian said, "and a great many things I want to buy you. But inevitably, since one can never keep anything completely quiet in France, our marriage is bound to be reported in the newspapers, and I will not have you worried or upset by journalists, or by anybody else for that matter."

"If we are going to Greece," Crisa said, "I cannot imagine anything more wonderful!"

"Of course we are going to Greece," he replied. "I want to see you in your proper environment. I want you to stand in Crisa, where your mother first thought of your name, and look up at the Shining Cliffs of Delphi and pray that the gods will go on being as kind to us as they have been up to now."

"They could not have given any woman a more . . . wonderful husband," Crisa whispered.

"And I could not find anywhere in the world a more beautiful, adorable, enchanting wife."

Once again, because the President was so grateful, he had lent them his private coach attached to the Express which was taking them to Marseilles, where they would board Adrian's private yacht to sail from there to Greece.

"A private yacht!" Crisa exclaimed when she heard of it. "Are you really so rich as to possess one?"

"Are you worried, after having disposed of your money in so many different ways, that you will find I am poverty-stricken?"

"No, of course not!" Crisa replied. "I sometimes wish you were as poor as I was with Papa when I used to worry about how to pay the bills and could not afford any luxuries. I would then look after you, and you would know how . . . very much I . . . love you."

"I know that already," Adrian said, "but as you have refrained from being inquisitive about my private affairs, I am prepared to tell you that I am in fact a rich man, and I intend to keep my promise, my darling, when we return home, to wrap you in sables and cover you in diamonds."

Crisa laughed.

"I want none of those things. I want horses to ride with you, and a home where I can look after you, and . . ."

She paused and hid her face against him.

"And?" he asked.

". . . and perhaps . . . one day we can have . . . lots of children who will . . . not be as lonely as I was."

She knew by the way Adrian's arms tightened that what she had said excited him.

Then, as she felt his arms around her, his lips on hers and his heart beating against her breast, she told herself that she would pray to give him sons as handsome as he was, and as kind and understanding.

After they had dined on the delicious food that had been served to them on the train, Crisa found the President's bed, which was very large and almost filled the whole compartment, very comfortable.

She was, however, thinking only that this was her wedding-night.

When they had knelt in front of the altar at the British Embassy Church, she had thought the whole place was filled with the presence of those she had loved and the celestial voices of angels.

She felt sure her father and mother were beside her, and that they were happy that she had found the same love that they had, and which would sustain her all her life.

She thought that other people who had married and prayed in the Church had left there the vibrations of their faith which came towards her now in the form of a blessing.

She hoped that Adrian could feel it, too, and as he put the ring on her finger and repeated the responses after the Clergyman in a firm, sincere voice, she was sure he was as moved as she was.

This was the supreme moment of their lives when, as he had said, he had found her again, and she had found him, and they would be together for all eternity.

Now, waiting for him with one light glowing beside the bed, she felt her love for him sweeping over her.

She knew that never again would she be frightened as she had been when she married Silas Vanderhault, and again when she had thought it impossible to escape from his relatives in New York.

"Thank You, God, thank You!" she prayed.

As she did so Adrian came in.

He was wearing a long dressing-gown with his initials surmounted by a coronet embroidered on the pocket.

She knew that no man could look so attractive, so distinguished, without the smart clothes and decorations he had worn when they were married.

He sat down on the bed, looking at her. Then he said:

"This is how I have wanted to see you. Your hair is just as lovely as I expected it would be, and your face is even more beautiful."

"That is . . . what I . . . want you to think," Crisa whispered. "Oh, darling, teach me how to . . . make you . . . happy and not to . . . fail you in . . . any way."

"How could you possibly do that?"

He kissed her hands, one by one, then pressed his lips on her palms.

Then as he got into the bed he said:

"Perhaps it seems rather strange to spend our first honeymoon night on a train. But everything we have done up to now has been both unconventional and original, so I suppose we should just accept it."

He moved closer and took Crisa in his arms.

"What does it matter . . . where we . . . are?" she asked. "When I was frightened on board ship I used to pretend that I was lying like this against you, and I knew then . . . although it did not seem possible . . . that somehow you would . . . save me."

"I have saved you, and you are never to be frightened again!"

"I should be frightened if you were ever . . . angry with me . . . or if you wanted to . . . leave me."

He laughed, and it was a very happy sound.

"Do you think that is possible? I feel I have fought a great number of unseen forces to make sure that you are mine. You see, I knew, my precious little love, because I could read your thoughts and because I love you, that something was wrong. Of course I could not guess what it was. How could I have imagined anything so fantastic? I just know that I had to make you trust me, to make you sure that we belonged to each other, and that our love is greater than anything else in the world."

"I was . . . stupid to be . . . afraid, and supposing I had run away . . . and you could . . . never find me?"

"I would have found you!" Adrian said firmly. "I would have found you if you had gone down to Hell itself, and now, my darling, I will never lose you and there is nothing and nobody to make you afraid."

Then he was kissing her; kissing her at first very gently, as if he wooed her, then a little more demandingly, until she felt little flashes of lightning moving through her body, and turning into flames.

It was so thrilling and so marvellous that she said incoherently:

"I . . . love you. Oh, my marvellous husband, teach me . . . about love . . . I am . . . frightened of . . . doing something . . . wrong."

"All you have to do, my precious, is to love me, but I am afraid of frightening you."

"How could I be . . . frightened of you . . . since when you touch me . . . and kiss me . . . it is like being in . . . Heaven?"

"That is what I want it to be, my darling."

Then as his kisses became more passionate, more demanding, Crisa felt her heart beating wildly, and it all seemed so incredible that the tears flooded into her eyes.

"You are not crying, my sweet?" Adrian asked, his voice deep and a little unsteady.

"Only because I am so rapturously . . . happy," Crisa answered. "I thought no-one would ever love me . . . because I was me."

Adrian drew her closer still as he said:

"Now you know I love you just as you are. All of you is mine—mine completely, and I have never owned anything so marvellous and so perfect."

As he spoke his hand moved over her breast and she felt the flames become more intense until she was burning with a fire that seemed to consume them both.

Then as their love carried them into the sky, they were enveloped with the light of Apollo, and as Adrian carried her up to the Shining Cliffs they were no longer human but one with the gods themselves.

ABOUT THE AUTHOR

Barbara Cartland, the world's most famous romantic novelist, who is also an historian, playwright, lecturer, political speaker and television personality, has now written over 430 books and sold over 400 million books the world over.

She has also had many historical works published and has written four autobiographies as well as the biographies of her mother and that of her brother, Ronald Cartland, who was the first Member of Parliament to be killed in the last war. This book has a preface by Sir Winston Churchill and has just been republished with an introduction by Sir Arthur Bryant.

Love at the Helm, a novel written with the help and inspiration of the late Admiral of the Fleet, the Earl Mountbatten of Burma, is being sold for the Mountbatten Memorial Trust.

Miss Cartland in 1978 sang an Album of Love Songs with the Royal Philharmonic Orchestra.

In 1976 by writing twenty-one books, she broke the world record and has continued for the following eight years with twenty-four, twenty, twenty-three, twenty-four, twenty-four, twenty-five, twenty-three, and twenty-six. She is in the *Guinness Book of Records* as the best-selling author in the world.

She is unique in that she was one and two in the Dalton List of Best Sellers, and one week had four books in the top twenty.

In private life Barbara Cartland, who is a Dame of the Order of St. John of Jerusalem, Chairman of the St. John Council in Hertfordshire and Deputy President of the St. John Ambulance Brigade, has also fought for better conditions and salaries for Midwives and Nurses.

Barbara Cartland is deeply interested in Vitamin Therapy and is President of the British National Association for Health. Her book *The Magic of Honey* has sold throughout the world and is translated into many languages. Her designs "Decorating with Love" are being sold all over the U.S.A., and the National Home Fashions League named her in 1981, "Woman of Achievement."

In 1984 she received at Kennedy Airport America's Bishop Wright Air Industry Award for her contribution to the development of aviation; in 1931 she and two R.A.F. Officers thought of, and carried, the first aeroplane-towed glider air-mail.

Barbara Cartland's Romances (a book of cartoons) has been published in Great Britain and the U.S.A., as well as a cookery book, *The Romance of Food,* and *Getting Older, Growing Younger*. She has recently written a children's pop-up picture book, entitled *Princess to the Rescue*.

More romance from
BARBARA CARTLAND

BARBARA CARTLAND

Called after her own
beloved Camfield Place,
each Camfield novel of love
by Barbara Cartland
is a thrilling, never-before published
love story by the greatest romance
writer of all time.